OUTNUMBERED
BUT NOT OUTGUNNED!

The other two nightriders saw him before the third did. Slocum let them rise from their chairs, even let them get their hands on the butts of their revolvers, before he fired. His aim proved to be as true as it ever had been. One bullet punched through the center of one nightrider's forehead, while another opened a hole in the other outlaw's chest, just above his heart . . .

DON'T MISS THESE
ALL-ACTION WESTERN SERIES
FROM THE BERKLEY PUBLISHING GROUP

THE GUNSMITH by J. R. Roberts
Clint Adams was a legend among lawmen, outlaws, and ladies. They called him . . . the Gunsmith.

LONGARM by Tabor Evans
The popular long-running series about U.S. Deputy Marshal Long—his life, his loves, his fight for justice.

LONE STAR by Wesley Ellis
The blazing adventures of Jessica Starbuck and the martial arts master, Ki. Over eight million copies in print.

SLOCUM by Jake Logan
Today's longest-running action western. John Slocum rides a deadly trail of hot blood and cold steel.

JAKE LOGAN

SLOCUM AND THE NIGHTRIDERS

BERKLEY BOOKS, NEW YORK

SLOCUM AND THE NIGHTRIDERS

A Berkley Book / published by arrangement with
the author

PRINTING HISTORY
Berkley edition / August 1993

ISBN: 0-425-13839-9

A BERKLEY BOOK ® TM 757,375
Berkley Books are published by The Berkley Publishing Group,
200 Madison Avenue, New York, New York 10016.
The name "BERKLEY" and the "B" logo
are trademarks belonging to Berkley Publishing Corporation.

PRINTED IN THE UNITED STATES OF AMERICA

10 9 8 7 6 5 4 3 2 1

SLOCUM AND THE NIGHTRIDERS

SLOCUM AND THE
NEIGHBORS

1

Slocum rode the dusty trail, the heat of the sun warm on his face. The spotted gelding beneath him plodded onward. The horse snorted. Its nostrils flared, drawing in the earthy odor of the crops around them and the distant scent of fresh water.

The tall drifter stared across the Kansas plains at the bounty that grew along either side of the trail. Wheat, barley, oats . . . all grew waist-deep and as far as the eye could see. Slocum nodded to himself. He could appreciate the effort that it took to raise crops such as these. He had farmed when he was a younger man. Slocum had felt the grit of earth on his hands and the sweat of labor on his brow; had plowed, planted, and harvested many an acre of corn, hay, and tobacco. But that had been years ago, before the war.

Slocum felt the gelding's urgency and let the horse travel of its own accord. A moment later he saw a lone farm standing amid the fields of grain. It was a simple farm: a single-story house, stock barn, and a few weathered outbuildings. A windmill stood beyond the barn. Its blades spun lazily in the late afternoon breeze.

He rode on until he reached a wire fence with a couple dozen head of cattle standing within its dusty, manure-littered yard. Most of the animals were beef cows, while a couple of Holsteins had obviously been reserved for milk and butter.

Slocum spotted a man working at the far end of the pen. His back was to the drifter as he nailed barbed wire to a sturdy corner post. Slocum studied the fellow as he neared the corral. The farmer was tall, his body bronzed by the sun and his muscles tight and hard. At first, Slocum figured the man to be in his forties, but his snow-white hair and beard revealed him to be perhaps fifteen or twenty years older. Even then, the farmer seemed to possess the stamina of a much younger man.

There was something else about the farmer that Slocum could not help but notice. His lean back was striped with long scars. The marks appeared to be fairly recent; the welps were pink and crusted with new scabs.

Slocum winced at the ugly scars. He thought of the marks that crisscrossed his own back. Slocum knew how it felt to be horsewhipped. His scars had been inflicted by a jailer many years ago, but the memory of the flogging remained fresh in his mind. He recalled the burn of the braided leather against his flesh, as well as the dirty laughter that had accompanied it and the sting of tobacco juice spat cruelly into the open wounds.

The tall man shook the thoughts from his mind and urged the gelding onward. He was not a man who enjoyed dwelling on the past, particularly a past as tragic as his own.

When he was within twenty feet of the stockyard, the farmer heard the drifter's approach and stopped his work. The iron hammer dropped from his hand, and before Slocum could react, the man grabbed up an old Henry rifle and whirled, aiming it from the hip.

Slate-gray eyes glared suspiciously from beneath bushy brows. "What do you want?" he asked gruffly.

Slocum rested his right hand on the horn of his saddle. It lay only a few inches from the curved butt of his Colt Navy, which jutted from a crossdraw holster at his waist. "Just passing through," he told the old man. "Was wondering if I could water my horse before I moved on."

The farmer was hesitant at first, his stern eyes appraising Slocum's face, as if trying to identify it. Finally, the man lowered the muzzle of his repeating rifle. "Do you hail from the South?" he asked.

"Georgia," replied Slocum. "What of it?"

The old man shrugged. "Just figured you for a son of Dixie. Could tell it from your voice. I'm formerly from Tennessee myself. Moved out here to Kansas when them damned carpetbaggers took over."

Slocum nodded. "It happened to a lot of men. What about that water?"

"Help yourself. The trough is on the far side of the barn there."

The tall rebel with the coal-black hair and the green eyes peered toward the west. "Is there a town nearby?" he asked.

"Tyler's Crossing," said the farmer. "About eight miles farther on. Wouldn't travel that distance after dark, though." An expression akin to fear flared in the old man's eyes for a second, then faded.

Slocum regarded the position of the sun. It was already past four o'clock. If it was eight miles to Tyler's Crossing, he would not be able to make it there before nightfall. From what he had gathered from the elderly farmer, there was some sort of danger along the Kansas trail and Slocum was certainly not one to look for trouble, even though it seemed to find him often enough.

"It'd be best if you stay the night here, young man," said the farmer, as if reading Slocum's mind. "Feel free to join me and my daughter for supper and sleep in the barn loft, if you want."

"I intend to pay you," Slocum told him flatly. "I'll give you a dollar in gold for my stay and oats for the gelding."

The farmer frowned thoughtfully. "Rather have some help mending this here fence."

Slocum was no stranger to hard work. "All right."

"My name's George Kelly," said the old man. "What should I call you?"

"John," replied the tall rebel.

"Just John? No last name?"

Slocum's expression darkened. "Is one necessary?"

"No," allowed Kelly. "I reckon that's your own business. Take care of your horse, then we'll get to work. We don't have but a couple more hours of daylight left."

Slocum rode on around the corner of the corral and toward the far side of the barn. He let the gelding drink its fill from the trough, then led the animal into the barn. He removed the saddle and slung it upon the wall of a stable, along with his rifle scabbard and saddlebags. He quickly rubbed down the horse, tossed some oats in a feeding trough, and left it tethered in an empty stall. Five other horses, all sturdy roans and mares, occupied the other stalls of the stock barn.

As the tall drifter left the barn, he nearly collided with a young woman who came around the corner from the direction of the chicken coop. Slocum's sudden appearance startled her, nearly causing her to drop a white hen that was undoubtedly destined for the supper table.

The woman took a step back, her eyes frightened. "Who are you?"

Slocum tipped his hat. "Name's John, ma'am. Mr. Kelly's letting me stay the night in return for some work."

The apprehension in the girl's lovely eyes faded and she smiled. "That's nice. Been a while since we've had company." The smile vanished for a second. "Decent company that is."

Slocum didn't know if decent was a word that best described him, particularly considering the feelings that the woman had just aroused in him. She was a pretty girl, perhaps in her early twenties, with curly brown hair and blue eyes as clear as the Kansas sky. She was something special to look at, especially for a man who had been alone on the trail for a couple of weeks. But Slocum wasn't sure he ought to be looking at the woman. It would be best if he just kept his thoughts to himself and steered clear of the girl.

"My name's Priscilla Kelly," she said. There was an expression of interest in her blue eyes that was vaguely teasing in nature. "Folks just call me Prissy, though." She moved past him, her eyes never leaving Slocum's own. "You go on out and help Pa, and I'll get supper started. Does chicken and dumplings and cornbread suit your taste?"

"Yes, ma'am," agreed Slocum. "Sounds fine."

Slocum watched as Prissy Kelly made her way to the farmhouse, then turned back to the corral and the work that awaited him there. He drove the girl from his mind. He thought of George Kelly and his Henry rifle, and knew it would not be worth the trouble getting involved with the farmer's daughter.

He joined Kelly at the fence, shedding his shirt and slipping on a pair of leather gloves he always carried with him. Slocum held the wicked strands of barbed wire against the posts while Kelly tacked them in place. Several times Slocum glanced toward the house and saw Prissy standing at the kitchen window, staring out at him. He tried to ignore her and keep his mind on his work, but it was difficult. It was hard for a man to keep his thoughts off a woman as beautiful as Prissy.

Slocum and George Kelly worked until the twilight of evening fell. They finished mending the fence just as Prissy rang the supper bell. The two men washed up at the horse trough, then walked on to the house, putting on their shirts. As they entered the back door of the farmhouse, they were greeted by the warm glow of coal-oil lanterns and the delicious aroma of the meal Prissy had prepared. Steaming pans of chicken and dumplings, garden vegetables, and sliced cornbread awaited them at the oak table.

Slocum waited until Kelly and his daughter had been seated, then sat down himself. He was about to grab for a bowl of butter beans, when Kelly announced "Let us say grace." Embarrassed by his lack of manners, Slocum mimicked the farmer and his daughter, bowing his head and clasping his hands. While Kelly voiced a prayer to the Lord Almighty, Slocum sat there feeling awkward. He had intended to ask the farmer if he had any whiskey after their meal was finished, but he dismissed that now, figuring that the elderly man was too God-fearing to keep liquor in his house.

When George Kelly had uttered the closing "Amen," both men attacked the table, revealing the ravenous hunger that the afternoon's work had bestowed upon them. Soon, their plates were heaped with food and they began to eat. Prissy served herself leisurely, beaming appreciatively at the men's hearty appetites.

Slocum was shoveling a forkful of chicken and dumplings into his mouth, when he felt something touch his leg beneath the table. At first he was startled, thinking maybe the Kellys had a pet dog or cat and that it was the animal that caressed his shin from ankle to knee. But glancing across the table, he came to the conclusion that it was Prissy who was to blame. He read a not-so-subtle expression in her eyes, an expression he had encountered in many women over the years. She wanted him, that was clear to see.

The tall rebel shifted uncomfortably in his chair. The girl's bare foot continued to run up and down his leg, making him hot and bothered. He glanced at George Kelly, but he seemed to be unaware of what was taking place beneath the shelter of the checkered tablecloth. The elderly farmer had his eyes centered on the mound of food on his plate. He worked the fork back and forth like a stableboy busily shoveling horse manure.

The meal went quietly. Slocum had found George Kelly to be a man of few words during their fence-mending, and the tall Georgian hadn't said much of anything himself, being pretty much cut from the same whole cloth. Slocum had almost come to the point of asking Kelly about the lash marks on his back several times, but decided to ask no questions. He figured it wasn't any of his business anyway.

When the meal was over, the men pushed away from the table, their bellies full. "Mighty good vittles, Miss Kelly," Slocum told her politely.

"Glad you enjoyed it," said Prissy. The young woman took her leave from the table. She gave the drifter one last bold look before hurriedly gathering up the dishes.

Slocum recalled the feel of the girl's foot rubbing his leg beneath the table and felt his arousal rise again. He left the table and turned toward the back door, hoping that Kelly didn't notice the bulge at the crotch of his trousers.

"I reckon you'll be heading for town in the morning," said Kelly.

Slocum nodded. "I'll be on the trail by dawn, more than likely."

"Much obliged for helping me with that fence," said Kelly. "Bobwire is mighty tricky to handle by one's self."

Slocum let himself out and closed the door behind him. He stood on the back porch of the farmhouse for a long moment, digging in his shirt pocket for the makings. He took the paper and tobacco, rolled himself a smoke, and lit it with a lucifer. Casting the sulfur match away, Slocum inhaled deeply, then started across the dirt yard toward the barn.

Halfway there, he turned and looked back at the house. He could see Prissy standing in the bright window of the kitchen. She smiled at him, but he looked away, deciding that it was best not to return the gesture. Slocum wanted no trouble with George Kelly. All he wanted was a good night's sleep and then to be on his way again at the first light of day.

2

Slocum's eyes snapped open when he heard a faint squeal echo through the musky darkness. He identified the sound at once; the rusty hinges of the barn door below. Someone was sneaking into the barn and was taking great pains to keep their approach as quiet as possible.

The tall drifter sat up from where he had made his bed in a mound of scattered hay. He reached toward a hay bale nearby. His hand immediately fisted around the handle of his Colt and he withdrew it. The Navy pistol and the six rounds in its engraved cylinder took some of the edge off the surprise visit, but not all of it. He wondered if perhaps George Kelly had noticed his daughter's bold attention toward Slocum and was coming to teach the tall Georgian a lesson for playing footsy underneath the supper table.

Slocum listened as the intruder entered the barn and closed the door. The darkness lifted as the yellow glow of a lantern invaded the roomy structure. He could hear soft footsteps crossing the earthen floor of the barn, but they were almost silent, not the heavy step and creaking leather of a man's boot. Then Slocum heard someone reach the ladder leading to the loft. Quietly the person mounted the rungs and began to climb, bringing the brightness of the lantern along.

Aiming his pistol at the top of the ladder and crisply cocking back the hammer, Slocum waited to see the bushy white head of George Kelly appear over the edge of the loft floor, as well as the muzzle of his Henry rifle. If that happened, Slocum figured it would be best to jump out of the hay door at the far end of the loft and make a run for it. The rebel had no beef with the farmer and would try to avoid trouble at any cost. He would rather make the jump than have to put a bullet in the elderly man.

He expected the worse, but it didn't come. Instead, Slocum received a pleasant surprise.

Prissy Kelly suddenly appeared at the top of the ladder. She stared at him for a moment, startled. Then she giggled. "You're not going to shoot me with that big hogleg of yours, are you, John? It wouldn't be very nice to shoot a perfect hostess like me."

Slocum eased the hammer down and returned the Colt to its holster. "Sorry," he said. He eyed the young woman uneasily. "So what are you doing here?"

Prissy climbed all the way into the hayloft, hanging the lantern on a crooked nail in a rafter overhead. "I thought maybe you might like a little company," said the woman. "And maybe a touch of this."

Slocum was surprised when she tossed him a bottle of whiskey.

"It's my father's," she told him. "He uses it for 'medicinal purposes.' I figured you to be a drinking man."

"You figured right." Slocum nodded. He uncorked the neck and tipped the bottle of red-eye, taking a long swallow. It wasn't the best whiskey he had drank, but then again it wasn't the worst either.

Prissy crossed the loft slowly, her white nightgown making her look like a graveyard ghost. "You know, I came here for another reason, too."

"I wonder what that could be?" mused Slocum. He knew very well why the girl had made her midnight visit.

Prissy moved in close to the drifter, wrapping her arms

around his neck. Slocum felt desire rise in his loins as the woman pressed her body against his. "Kiss me, John. I want you to kiss me."

Slocum obliged, meshing his lips with her own. The kiss was long and lingering. Teasingly, Prissy slipped her tongue past his teeth.

Kelly and his rifle intruded on Slocum's thoughts again and he pulled away. "What about your father?" he asked the girl.

Prissy grinned mischievously. "Aw, he ain't gonna find out. Pa sleeps like a winter grizzly. A Texas twister couldn't wake him up if it came right up to the house and knocked on the front door."

Slocum wasn't too certain. "I don't know about this, Prissy."

The brunette's eyes flashed hungrily. Her hand reached down and grabbed the bulge of his britches. Her fingers kneaded him like biscuit dough. "I want you, John. I want to feel you inside me. Please, don't make me beg. I'd rather not, but I will if I have to."

Slocum felt his control slipping. He had to know something first, though. "Be honest with me. Are you—?"

Prissy laughed. "A virgin? No, I've done it before. But only with farmboys with hair triggers. Never had me a real honest to goodness man before."

Slocum could stand it no longer. "You'll have your chance at one now," he whispered huskily. He gathered the long skirt of her gown in his hands, then lifted it over her head. Her body was revealed in the glow of the lantern, the skin as white as porcelain, the hair between her legs dark and downy. He reached down and ran his fingers along her opening. She was damp and ready for him.

Prissy quickly undressed Slocum, until he, too, was naked. When the drifter began to pull her onto the bed of straw,

Prissy giggled. "No, I want to do it myself. I want to ride you."

Slocum gave Prissy her way. He reclined in the hay and watched as the woman straddled him. The touch of her soft skin against him was maddening. Prissy took his prick in her hand and guided him in. Slocum groaned as liquid warmth engulfed his rigid member.

The brunette moaned herself as she began to work her hips, slowly at first, then faster and faster. Slocum reached up and took her breasts in his hands. He ran his thumbs across her hardened nipples, bringing new groans of pleasure from the woman. He bucked up as she rocked downward. The two met with hard, wet slaps.

Abruptly Slocum took the reins. He grabbed Prissy's ass and flipped her over. "Yes," urged the girl. "Drive it in me! Drive it in deep!"

Slocum spread Prissy's legs wide and went at it. His prick was like a piston as he rutted like a horny buck. He held that position for as long as he could, knowing that he couldn't hold out forever. Finally, he felt his sap rising. Slocum and Prissy came at the same time. They restrained their screams of passion, fearing that they might awaken Prissy's father. Then, physically drained, both settled into the hay, their breathing heavy and their bodies bathed in the sweat of exertion.

The tall Southerner sat up and took a swallow from the whiskey bottle that sat on a hay bale. As he drank, Prissy stretched lazily and traced the marks on Slocum's body with an inquisitive finger. She went from one to the next; the belly scar from a knife fight in Soccorro, the whip lashes across his back, and, of course, the puckered bullet wound on his upper chest, inflicted by those he had unwillingly ridden with during the War Between the States.

Prissy pursed her pretty lips in a frown. "So sad," she

whispered. "Such a handsome man with so much ugliness on his body."

"Every man has scars," said Slocum. "Your father has his."

Prissy's blue eyes began to well up with tears. "Yes, dammit," she cursed. "He does."

Slocum set the bottle of red-eye aside. "Who did it, Prissy? Who horsewhipped your pa?"

Prissy turned her eyes toward Slocum. Sorrow and fear were there, but there was also a generous amount of anger. Whoever had taken a whip to her father had made an enemy of her for life. Slocum had seen such raw hatred in men's eyes before—he had possessed such a rage himself at times. But never had he seen such fierce emotion generate from a face as angelic and beautiful as Prissy Kelly's.

The young woman was about to tell Slocum what he wanted to know, when the drumming of horses' hooves sounded from the trail next to the Kelly farm. Man and woman sat in the loft, straining to hear the commotion that burst into the barnyard below. They heard shouts and dirty laughter, then the crash of a door violently kicked inward. It was the back door of the Kelly house.

"Oh, Lord, no," gasped Prissy. "It's them. They're back!"

Ironically, John Slocum knew that his question concerning George Kelly had just been answered.

The elderly farmer was sound asleep when the back door of his farmhouse crashed inward under the forceful heel of a boot. He was a heavy sleeper, but this noise cut through his slumber and shook him into wakefulness.

Kelly was climbing out of his bed, intending to retrieve the Henry rifle from where it leaned in the corner, when a dark form appeared in the doorway of his bedroom. The man was big and burly, and dressed entirely in black from

his high-peaked hat to his dusty riding boots. Even the big
Colt Dragoon in the invader's gloved hand looked as black
as sin and twice as deadly.

"Hold it right there, old man," the intruder warned. His
voice was muffled by a black kerchief that masked his lower
face. "Take another step toward that Henry and I'll put a hole
right through you!"

George Kelly decided that it was best to forget the lever-
action. He had dealt with these men before and knew they
weren't ones for bluffing. "Get out of here, you son of a
bitch," he demanded defiantly. "Get off my property and
leave me be!"

The big fellow crossed the floor and grabbed Kelly roughly
by the front of his nightshirt. "Afraid that ain't our job, you
old codger," rasped the man. He pressed the muzzle of the
big horse pistol beneath Kelly's bearded jaw. "Our job is
to teach you and them other sodbusters the law of Tyler's
Crossing. And it looks like you didn't learn very well the
last time we came calling."

With scarcely any effort at all, the man in black hustled
Kelly out of his house and into the moonlit barnyard. The
farmer was slung to the ground, where he lay on his back for
a moment, catching his breath and staring up at the horsemen
who surrounded him.

The band of nightriders were just as ominous as they had
been a week earlier. Each man was decked out in ebony
clothing and sat in the dark saddle of an equally black horse.
All wore black scarfs to conceal their lower faces, while the
shadows of their broad-brimmed hats hid their eyes from
view. There were twelve in all, tall, sturdy men with an
air of danger about them. Most carried revolvers, rifles, and
scatterguns, held at the ready, the hands holding them itching
to put them to use. Only one man held no weapon. Instead,
he clutched a coiled length of braided bullwhip.

"You know why we're here, Kelly," said the man with the Dragoon. He had a way of authority that pegged him as the leader of the bunch. "The Judge was waiting for you to come sign those papers day before yesterday. You didn't show up."

"Damn you!" grated Kelly. "Damn you all! It'll be a cold day in hell when I give in to the likes of you."

The boss nightrider turned and looked around at his confederates. "Stubborn old cuss, ain't he?" His observation was answered with amused laughter. "I reckon he needs some more persuading." The leader nodded to the lanky rider who held the bullwhip. "Ten more lashes than the last time. And this time cut 'em clear down to the bone!"

The wielder of the whip motioned to two other riders. Silently he climbed from his dark stallion as his helpers wrestled the old man to his feet. Soon, they had taken a length of rawhide and bound his wrists to the sturdy rail of a hitching post. The tall nightrider walked calmly to Kelly and, with one swipe of his gloved hand, ripped the nightshirt completely off the elderly man. The farmer was completely exposed now. His naked back and buttocks seemed as pale as lard in the light of the Kansas moon.

The tall rider regarded Kelly for a long moment, his eyes almost lustful with sadistic glee. Teasingly he let the end of the bullwhip move gently down the curve of Kelly's spine, ending at the cleft of his ass. Then he turned toward the leader of the gang, awaiting further instructions.

"Let him have it," said the nightrider who held the .44 Dragoon in his hand.

Gracefully the tall man turned back to the naked farmer. Cruel laughter rumbled from beneath his mask as he raised the bullwhip at arm's length, eager to perform the task that he was so adept at.

3

Slocum crouched beside the open door of the hayloft that looked down upon the barnyard below. He fastened his trousers and buckled his gunbelt as he watched the leader of the dark riders drag George Kelly bodily from his house and fling him to the ground.

Prissy Kelly knelt next to Slocum, having slipped back into her gown and joined him at the hay door. Terror filled her eyes as she stared at the assemblage of nightriders that surrounded her father. "Oh, dear God, don't let them do it again," she whispered tearfully.

Slocum studied the man in black. They were trouble, that was plain to see, and the tall rebel tried to avoid trouble at all costs. Whatever trouble George and Prissy Kelly were involved in, it was no business of his. However, Slocum did have a conscience, no matter how much of a hard case he might be. And there was no way in hell he could remain there silently and watch the old man suffer the agony and humiliation of being horsewhipped a second time. He understood how that form of punishment felt and how it wounded a man mentally as well as physically.

"Bring me my rifle," he told Prissy. "It's in the stable with my gear."

Quietly the woman obeyed his request, easing down the loft ladder to the barn floor. Slocum turned back to the

16

scene unfolding before him. Two of the nightriders were dragging Kelly to a hitching post. He watched as they tied his hands securely to the rail. Slocum reached down to his holster and ran a hand over the curved butt of his Colt Navy. He could probably stop the riders with his six-gun alone, but he would feel better holding the Winchester .44-40 in his hands. It was more accurate from such a distance.

Prissy returned a moment later. Slocum worked the Winchester's lever as quietly as possible. Then, raising the rifle to his shoulder, he turned its sights on the band of riders below.

The skinny fellow with the bullwhip had dismounted his coal-black roan and approached the hitching post. Slocum grimaced as the man ripped the nightshirt from George Kelly's body and cruelly ran the tip of the whip down his naked back. He knew that the man was laughing beneath his mask, even though Slocum was too far away to hear. Men like him always laughed; they derived a sadistic thrill from inflicting pain.

"Well, not this time," rasped Slocum beneath his breath. He waited until the whipmaster raised his hand to lash out, then took careful aim. Slocum waited until just the right moment, then squeezed off a single shot.

The rifle slug ripped through the back of the nightrider's hand and exited his palm, shattering the wooden haft of the bullwhip he held. The man did not yell out. He cursed softly and clutched at his wounded hand, turning his gaze toward the dark window of the hayloft. The whipmaster's eyes glittered in the moonlight. Even from that distance, Slocum could see the meanness there, cold and contemptuous. They were like the eyes of a rattler ready to strike.

Slocum wasted no time. He jacked the lever-action once again and swept the muzzle from left to right, covering the dark dozen, watching for threatening movement. "Untie him," he called out.

"Who are you?" demanded the leader. He held his Colt Dragoon in his right hand, relaxed, but at the ready.

Something about the man bothered Slocum. His voice sounded oddly familiar to the tall Georgian. There was also something about the man's broad build and the way he had fastened holstered pistols to either side of his saddle that nagged at Slocum's mind. A memory almost surfaced, but Slocum pushed it aside, centering his attention on the situation below instead.

"It doesn't matter who I am," he replied. "Now head out before I shoot again."

"Like hell!" growled a potbellied rider toting a twelve-gauge Parker. The fellow lifted the shotgun into line and thumbed back the twin hammers.

Slocum took aim and fired. The nightrider's left knee opened in a bloody blossom as the slug found its mark. With a shriek, the fat rider tumbled from his saddle. He hit hard on his back, both barrels of the shotgun discharging harmlessly into the night sky.

"You'd best do as I say and go," Slocum warned them for the last time. "Take it from me, my next shot will be to kill and not to wound."

The band of nightriders shifted uncomfortably, their voices mumbling in low discussion. It appeared that most of them were itching to rush the barn and smoke out the sniper in the hayloft. But the leader refused to allow it. He stared at the dark opening near the peak of the barn, knowing very well that he would probably be the rifleman's next target if any move was made against the structure.

"Cut him loose," the head rider said angrily, reluctant to give in to the sniper's demand.

"But what will the Judge say?" asked one of the men.

"Who gives a damn? He ain't out here with a rifle pointed at his head. Now get down off that horse and cut Kelly loose."

The nightrider did as he was told. Soon, Kelly had been freed of his bonds. The farmer slumped to the dusty ground, glaring hatefully at the dark men gathered around him. If looks could kill, they would have all died a slow and agonizing death.

"Let's head out," called the leader. He waited until the injured men had remounted, then turned toward the barn. "Whoever you are, you've bought yourself a mess of trouble. If we ever find out who you are, we're gonna give you a taste of the whip."

Slocum shifted his aim toward the ground and fired. The bullet kicked up dirt between the hooves of the leader's horse. The stallion reared and bucked. The man with the Dragoon fought to stay in the saddle and finally succeeded in calming his mount. With a curse, the nightrider turned and, spurring the flanks of his horse, headed back down the trail. The others swiftly followed.

The tall drifter watched as the riders vanished into the night. He breathed a sigh of relief and jacked the spent shell from the breech. "Go see to your father," he told Prissy.

Slocum finished dressing as Prissy left the barn and helped her elderly father to his feet. From the way he acted, it was clear to see that George was unaware that Prissy had even been away from the farmhouse. He was too shaken by the nightriders' invasion to think otherwise.

Slocum stood in the open doorway of the hayloft, staring across the dark plains toward the west. The voice of the lead nightrider echoed in his mind. He was certain that he recognized that voice from somewhere. But, try as he may, Slocum couldn't say exactly who in his past it had belonged to.

• • •

Prissy Kelly sat a cup of hot coffee in front of her father. "Are you sure you're all right, Pa?" she asked with concern.

"No need to fuss so much over me, daughter," said the old man gruffly. "I've endured anything you could think of during my lifetime . . . flood, drought, Yankees, and injuns. A few low-down bushwhackers sure ain't going to bring me down."

Prissy seemed to calm down in the face of her father's brave talk, but Slocum could sense the fear underneath. He noticed the trembling of Kelly's hand when he raised the china cup to his mouth and took a long sip of the hot coffee.

George Kelly looked across the table at the tall drifter. "I owe you a debt of gratitude for running those scoundrels off, John. I'm beholden to you." Kelly searched Slocum's eyes, looking for a trace of interest. "I reckon you're curious as to what it was all about."

"No, sir," admitted Slocum truthfully. "I'd just soon as not know about it. All I want is to get a few more hours sleep, then be on my way at dawn."

Prissy planted her hands on her hips and stared at the man incredulously. "You mean to tell me that you're not interested in our trouble at all?"

Slocum directed his gaze at the cup in his hands. "No, ma'am, I'm not. I reckon a man has more than his share of trouble without looking for it. And I'd rather not get involved in someone else's."

"Oh, that's a fine attitude to have!" said Prissy, her pretty blue eyes full of hurt. "That's why the nightriders are getting away with it! Because folks don't want to step in and take some responsibility."

Slocum downed the rest of his coffee and stood up. "Like I said before, I'd rather not hear the details."

"Can't say that I blame John," Kelly told his daughter. "This ain't his affair. Anyway, I've always handled my own strife and I ain't about to ask for help now."

Slocum said good-bye to George Kelly, then left the farmhouse, intending to return to the loft and get as much shut-eye as possible before morning. He was almost to the barn when he heard Prissy's voice call out to him.

"Wait!" she called. Slocum turned to see her running toward him. She stopped before him and held out a small pouch. "Here."

Slocum heard the jingle of coins and refrained from taking the purse. "What is it?"

"Fifty dollars in gold," Prissy told him. "All the money I have in this world."

"I don't understand," said Slocum, although he was beginning to see what she was driving at.

"I want to hire you to protect me and my father against those horrible men," Prissy said. "I saw how you handled that rifle. A man doesn't become that skilled unless he's made a trade of it."

Slocum turned back toward the barn. "I'm no hired gun, Prissy," he said stonily. "Now, if you'll excuse me, I've got some sleep to catch up on."

Angrily Prissy grabbed Slocum's arm. "How can you act so cold toward me? Especially after what we shared tonight?"

The remark sent a pang of guilt through Slocum. He recalled the pleasure they had enjoyed together, but then he had shared the same with other women over the years. He tried hard to convince himself that Prissy Kelly was no exception. "I'm sorry, Prissy, but what we did tonight . . . that's as far as it goes."

"Oh, I see," said the woman haughtily. "You just take a poke at me, then ride off. It must be nice, to do as you please and then move on, as if nothing happened."

Slocum turned away from the brunette. "Good night, Prissy," he said and again started for the barn.

Prissy Kelly said nothing else. She turned and stalked angrily back to the farmhouse.

Slocum entered the barn and returned to his bed in the hayloft. He lay there, awake, for a long while, unable to go to sleep. He kept thinking of the Kellys and Prissy in particular. What did they expect of him? He had done the decent thing and driven the nightriders away that night. They had no right to expect him to get involved in trouble that wasn't his own.

Slocum fell to sleep convincing himself of that fact, but a part of him felt badly about it. Secretly he wanted to help Prissy and her father, but he knew that it would only put him in danger once again. Slocum knew, sooner or later, that annoying habit of his would end up putting him six feet underground.

And he wasn't about to make that sacrifice if he could possibly avoid it.

4

The sun was two hours high in the Kansas sky when Slocum rode into the town of Tyler's Crossing.

He reined his horse to a halt at the eastern end of town and surveyed the settlement for a moment. Tyler's Crossing was similar to a hundred other towns the Southerner had passed through. A single main street of packed earth and hardened horse manure separated the balconied buildings and false-fronted shops into two rows. There was a huge livery barn constructed of weathered lumber and rusted tin at one end of town, while a two-story courthouse of red brick and whitewashed wood stood at the other. Slocum figured the tall, stately building to be something of a peculiarity amid the rest of the drab and familiar structures. It somehow seemed out of place there in that small farming community.

Slocum recalled something that he had heard the lead nightrider say the night before. He had mentioned someone called the Judge. Maybe that was who had built the brick building at the end of the main street. Slocum had encountered a few pompous, self-important judges in his time and most considered themselves a hairbreadth short of God when it came to laying down the law and setting standards in the community they had been assigned to.

The incident of the previous night turned Slocum's thoughts back to George Kelly and his daughter. Slocum had done just what he had vowed to do. At the first hint of dawn, the drifter

23

had his gear packed and his gelding saddled. As he was leading the animal into the barnyard, he caught the enticing scents of biscuits baking and sugar-cured ham sizzling in the pan. He had glanced toward the kitchen window of the Kelly house and seen Prissy staring at him through the glass. But she had merely pulled the curtains shut and gone on about her business, neglecting to invite him to stay for breakfast. Slocum had been half angered and half relieved by the rebuff. He had mounted his horse and, without a second glance, left the farmstead and hit the trail for town.

But two hours of steady riding with only a quiet horse and a growling stomach to keep him company had made him realize what a comfort that parting meal at the Kellys would have been. He cursed himself for being a fool, then guided his horse toward the livery.

The clink and clang of a mallet against hot steel echoed from the lean-to at the side of the barn. Slocum climbed down from the saddle and tethered his horse to a rail outside, then walked over. A burly man in a long leather apron leaned over a large anvil, shaping horseshoes. He caught Slocum's approach out of the corner of his eye and turned, taking a short break from his work. "Help you with something, mister?"

"Need to put up my horse for a day or two," said Slocum. "How much?"

"Two bits a day," said the blacksmith. "Three if you want him fed oats instead of hay."

Slocum dug into his pocket, then laid six bits atop the anvil. "Any place around here where I can get some breakfast?"

"Your best bet would be over at the saloon," said the big man. "They serve red-eye gravy and cat-head biscuits for free if you buy whiskey. There's Miss Belamy's boardinghouse, but she's a stiff-necked churchgoer and doesn't like rough types or saddle tramps. No offense, of course."

"None taken," assured Slocum. "I'll try my luck at the saloon."

"I'll take good care of that gelding for you," said the liveryman. "Name's Hinchburger. I do work for pert near everyone in town. Even the Judge."

"Judge?" asked Slocum, trying not to appear too curious.

"Judge Harrison Burke," said Hinchburger. The smithy's eyes hardened a bit. "You'd do well to steer clear of the Judge while in town, mister. The Judge has a cruel streak to him and he don't much cotton to strangers in his town, even those who are passing through. Just thought I'd warn you."

"Obliged for the advice," said Slocum. He took his rifle and saddlebags from the gelding and crossed the street, heading in the direction of the saloon.

The drinking establishment was a two-story structure named the Plowman Saloon and obviously catered to the hard-working farmers who gave the watering hole most of its regular business. When Slocum stepped into the wide room with its sawdust floor, tables and chairs, long walnut bar, and tarnished brass spittoons, he glanced up at the upper floor where a balcony encircled it on three sides. The second story more than likely housed rooms for rent or permanent lodging for the soiled doves who plied their trade to lonely drifters or drunken farmers who had come into town for supplies and gotten sidetracked with a bottle of whiskey or a game of faro.

Slocum walked to the bar. A gaunt, dark-haired bartender with the look and demeanor of a mortician stood at the far end, reading a dime novel about Wild Bill Hickok. In the center of the bar sat a platter piled high with big buttermilk biscuits and a steaming bowl of red-eye gravy. The smell of the vittles sent Slocum's belly into a renewed fit of growling.

"Fella named Hinchburger sent me over," he told the bartender. "Said you'd offer a man breakfast for the price of a drink."

"That's right." The man nodded, lifting his somber eyes from the pages of the booklet.

"Then I'll take a bottle and eat my fill." Slocum tossed a gold piece on the counter.

The bartender was none too slow about picking up the coin. He snatched it off the bar and brought a bottle of whiskey and a shot glass from a shelf underneath. "Help yourself," he invited, then returned to his reading.

Slocum stood at the bar and quelled his hunger pains, alternating between shots of whiskey and bites of biscuit and gravy. While he ate, Slocum was aware of movement on the balcony above. He glanced up and saw a tall, buxom blonde leave one of the upstairs rooms. The saloon girl was dressed in a gaudy costume of pink silk and black lace, and her oval face was laden with paint and powder. Still, she exuded a natural beauty that showed through the flashy clothing and heavy makeup.

As Slocum turned back to the platter of food, the woman descended the stairs and regarded the dark-haired Southerner with admiration. "It does my heart good to see a man eat like that," she said, moving across the barroom with the grace of a cat. "Of course, there are certain appetites that food and liquor can't satisfy."

Slocum knew the kind of appetite that the whore was talking about, but he was more concerned with his stomach at that moment than any other part of his anatomy. He poured himself another shot of whiskey and sopped another biscuit into the red-eye gravy.

"Leave the man be, Charlene," said the bartender. "Besides, I'd think you'd be all tuckered out, all the whooping and hollering I heard coming from your room last night."

"Why don't you stick that pointed nose of yours back into that dime novel and mind your own business, Henry," said the woman. "What about it, stranger? Do you want me to scat or would you like a little company with your breakfast?"

"Don't make no difference to me," said Slocum around a mouthful of food. "Stay if you want."

"A hard case, huh?" asked Charlene with a frown. "Well, I must admit, I've met my share of 'em. I reckon you ain't any different than any of the others."

Slocum shrugged. "I reckon not."

Charlene leaned against the bar next to him. When she reached out for the whiskey bottle, Slocum made no effort to stop her. She poured a shot into the Southerner's glass and took a long, lingering sip. "What's your name, handsome?"

"John," said Slocum. He paused for a moment, then continued. "John Smith."

The whore laughed. "Oh, yes, I've met quite a few John Smiths since I came out here from Philadelphia. Are you running from the law or do you just want to be left alone?"

Slocum regarded her with a half smile, his piercing green eyes meeting her violet-blue ones. "Maybe a little of both."

"You plan on staying here in Tyler's Crossing long?"

Slocum poured himself another whiskey. "A day or two, then back on the trail again." He nodded to a table in a far corner of the saloon. "I'm tired of standing here. Will you join me?"

Charlene smiled, flashing perfect teeth. "Why not?"

Slocum bought another bottle of whiskey from the bartender, then the drifter and the saloon girl retired to the corner table. Slocum removed the cork with his teeth, then poured both of them a drink.

"Which direction are you coming from, John?" asked Charlene. "East or west?"

"East," Slocum allowed, figuring it would do no harm to tell her.

"Then you probably passed by the Kelly farm. You didn't happen to see anything, did you? I heard there was trouble out there last night."

Slocum figured it would be best not to mention his brief visit at the Kelly place. "No, I rode straight here from Salina. Haven't stopped much of anywhere since I left."

The drifter hoped that Charlene would continue with the subject and she didn't disappoint him. "There's some bad business going on here in Tyler's Crossing. Between Judge Burke and some of the farmers hereabouts. The Judge claims they owe him back taxes and they claim he's just trying to rob them of their earnings come harvesttime."

"Who do you think is in the right?" asked Slocum.

Charlene cast a glance over at Henry, then lowered her voice. "Frankly, I side with the farmers, but I'd never breathe a word of that to anyone. The Judge has about as many hired ears around this town as he does hired guns." She suddenly eyed Slocum suspiciously. "That isn't what you're here for, is it?"

Slocum reached down and patted the butt of his Colt Navy. "This is for my use alone. I don't hire it out to nobody."

Charlene relaxed a little. "Anyway, I've heard tell that the farmers have been getting some unwelcome visitors in the dead of night. Riders in black. And I saw a couple of the farm women bring their men to the doctor here in town. They were all busted up and I know for sure one was horsewhipped. Makes my skin crawl, thinking someone would do such a thing for the sake of greed."

"So you figure the Judge is behind it?"

The blonde shrugged and poured another drink. "I'm not saying for sure, but it sure seems peculiar. The Judge's newly appointed sheriff, Hicks, and a dozen of his so-called deputies disappear whenever those nightriders go on one of their rides."

The mention of the name got Slocum to wondering again. He recalled how the head rider's voice had sounded naggingly familiar to him. And now the name of Hicks had reinforced that feeling, made it even stronger than before. "Who did you say?" he asked, just to make sure.

"Hicks," she replied. "Some loudmouthed, white-trash Missourian named Luther Hicks." Charlene sat with her back to the wall, her lovely eyes directed toward the saloon door. As Slocum heard the squeal of rusty hinges behind him, Charlene's gaze faltered and she lowered her eyes a degree. "Speaking of the devil . . ."

Slocum turned his head enough to see several men enter the Plowman Saloon. All seemed weary from lack of sleep, a couple of them yawning openly. The man at the forefront— a big bear of a man with a high-peaked hat, sheriff's badge, and a Colt Dragoon holstered on his right hip—led the way to the bar, where the bunch bought whiskey and then hungrily attacked the heaping platter of biscuits and gravy.

Suddenly the connection was made between voice, name, and the man's physical appearance. It took all of Slocum's willpower to restrain himself from stepping away from the table and drawing his Navy pistol. For he knew the burly man named Luther Hicks and he possessed a deep hatred for the man. A hatred that was understandable, given the dire wrong he had done Slocum during those bloody years when North and South had clashed so very violently.

5

True, Luther Hicks looked a little different from the time in which Slocum had known him, but the Georgian still recognized the man. He looked like he had gained a good thirty pounds and he now wore a heavy beard, where he had only worn a mustache before. The jagged scar across his left cheek—put there by a Union cavalryman's saber—was still the same, as were the man's eyes. They were still as cold and gray as a well stone, with the faintest glint of pure meanness lurking way back in the depths of them.

Sitting there at that barroom table in the Plowman Saloon, John Slocum recalled the last time he had seen those cruel eyes staring down at him. The spring of '65; a time of drunken laughter, the sharp crack of gunfire, and searing pain. Unconsciously Slocum raised a hand to his chest where the old bullet wound lay beneath his shirt. Luther Hicks hadn't put it there, but he had been there when the shot had been fired.

Slocum felt his body lock with tension as he fought with his emotions, trying to put a steady rein on them. He listened to the men talk as they ate and heard Hicks's coarse laughter. He closed his eyes and gripped the neck of the whiskey bottle so tightly that his knuckles grew white.

"What's the matter, John?" asked Charlene. There seemed to be genuine concern in the woman's voice.

Slocum breathed deeply, then opened his eyes. He forced a

smile. "Nothing," he told her. He tipped the bottle of red-eye and poured himself another shot.

Charlene looked doubtful, but didn't press the matter.

The Southerner grew silent. He and the fallen angel drank quietly for a while, saying nothing. Slocum drove his thoughts away from times past, knowing that a confrontation with Hicks might prove fatal. During those days of war, Slocum had been a master sniper; no one could hold a candle to him when it came to handling a Sharps rifle or Spencer carbine. Hicks, however, was a fast hand with the six-shooter. He was lightning quick and faultless of aim when it came to using those hogleg Colts of his. He had knocked many a Yankee cavalryman from the saddle with the roar of those .44-caliber Dragoons.

Slocum was not a man to run from a fight, but he was also smart enough to know when he should take care and avoid one. It was likely that Hicks's skill with a revolver had only increased with time, and despite Slocum's feelings toward the man, he knew it would be wise to bide his time and think on whether or not he should confront Hicks about what had taken place in that lonely stretch of Missouri woods so many years ago.

The drifter sat there, straining to hear what the men were talking about.

"Still can't figure who it was?" said a short fellow with red hair and dark freckles. "I mean, he shot like a professional, that's for sure. Got both Baxter and Guthrie where it hurts the most."

"Baxter's out for sure," said Luther Hicks. "That rifle shot tore his knee all to hell. Likely to be a cripple from now on."

"And what about Guthrie's hand?" asked a lanky man with greasy black hair.

"I talked to Doc Hunter. He said the wound was clean

enough. The bullet didn't hit any bones, just nicked the muscles if anything. Guthrie's hand will be stiff for a while, but that don't matter. He can handle that whip just as well with his other one."

"Do you think Old Man Kelly hired himself a gun?" asked the redhead.

"Don't know," said the sheriff. "But I reckon we oughtta steer clear of the Kelly place for a while and concentrate more on the others."

Slocum hoped to hear some mention of the Judge, but Hicks and his deputies neglected to include him in their conversation.

"Well, to hear them talking it seems like my suspicions were right," whispered Charlene. "They are behind what's been going on."

Slocum shrugged nonchalantly. "Ain't no affair of mine," he told her.

"No," said Charlene, taking another sip of whiskey. "Mine neither." She eyed the Southerner curiously. "Are your appetites settled now or are you still hungry? Perhaps there's something I can do for you?"

Slocum smiled. "Maybe later."

Charlene returned the smile. "All right. But in the meantime, I've got to earn my keep. Don't mean to be rude or anything . . ."

"Go on," said Slocum. "Business is business."

The saloon girl winked at the drifter, then left the table. Putting an exaggerated swagger into her hips, Charlene sauntered over to the bar and parked herself between the short redhead and the skinny, dark-haired fellow. Soon, her charms had worked their magic and the men had lost interest in their breakfast of gravy and biscuits.

When Slocum was halfway through the second bottle of whiskey, a chubby fellow dressed in a black frockcoat and gray derby hat walked in. Slocum watched as the man went to a table covered with green felt, removed his coat and hat, and donned red sleeve garters and a gambler's shade. The dark-haired Georgian had a weakness for games of chance. He left his table and walked over to where the fat man was setting up shop.

"Just name your game, sir," said the gambler. "Faro, blackjack, dice . . . it's your choice."

"Poker," said Slocum. He pulled out a chair and began to sit down.

"That sounds good to me," boomed a familiar voice from the direction of the bar.

Slocum turned to see Luther Hicks heading toward the gambling table with a bottle of whiskey in his hand. Slocum felt himself stiffen again, ready to make a move. But he didn't. He fought off the urge, acting as if he didn't even know the man.

As the big man parked himself across the table from Slocum, the gambler broke out the chips and a crisp, new deck of playing cards. "Best watch ol' Flanders here, stranger," said Hicks. "He tends to deal from the bottom when his luck plays out."

"Don't listen to him," said Flanders, looking hurt. "My reputation is a sterling one, sir. I've dealt honest everywhere from Dodge City to Deadwood. Even spent a couple of years on a Mississippi riverboat."

Slocum had traveled the river before and had himself gambled on many a paddlewheel. Most captains allowed only the cream of the crop to work their casinos, knowing that cheats and cardsharps would eventually bring trouble and dishonor, two things that most river pilots tried their best to avoid.

As Flanders cut the deck, Hicks introduced himself. "I'm Luther Hicks, the sheriff here in Tyler's Crossing. What's your name?"

"John Smith," replied Slocum.

Hicks smiled and nodded. "Yeah, I get you." The cards were dealt and the game began. "You looking for work, Smith?" Hicks asked after tossing a couple of disfavorable pasteboards aside.

"Why do you ask?" Slocum replied. He kept his attention glued to his cards.

"I don't know," said Hicks. "Seems like a man who carries a Colt in a crossdraw holster the way you do and totes a .44-40 Winchester might want to make himself some money. Good money."

"As a gunman, you mean?"

Hicks laid his cards facedown on the table long enough to pluck a cigar from his vest pocket and light it with a lucifer. "Yeah, that's what I'm getting at. Except you'd be considered more of a deputy than anything else."

Slocum eyed his cards, then bet a dollar. "And I reckon you'd know where such a job could be had?"

Hicks matched the drifter's bet. "That's right," he said. He pulled the cigar from his yellowed teeth long enough to blow a perfect smoke ring. "We're always in need of men like you here in Tyler's Crossing, Smith."

Slocum showed his hand. "Full house," he announced to the disgust of Flanders and Hicks. "Sorry, Sheriff, but I'm no hired gun, deputy or otherwise. I'm just resting up here for a couple of days before I head on to Colorado."

Luther Hicks eyed Slocum with a suspicious eye as Flanders collected the cards and began to shuffle them again. "If you ain't a handy man with a gun, then I'm Marshal Wyatt Earp. But, hey, I ain't gonna argue with you none." He reached into his pocket and brought out a roll of crumpled greenbacks. "Now let's play us some serious poker. I'm aiming to win back what I lost to that full house of yours."

"We'll see about that," said Slocum. The smile he wore was tight and humorless, matching the coldness in his eyes.

Four hands later, Slocum left the gambling table. He stuffed forty dollars he had won off Hicks into his shirt pocket and savored the dark mood that the sheriff had slipped into after losing to Slocum four times in a row. "Enjoyed playing against you," he said truthfully.

Hicks chewed on the butt of his cigar. "Yeah. I'll see you around, Smith."

Slocum walked over to the bar where Henry was still reading his dime novel. The lanky fellow with the oily hair was still there, finishing up the last of the saloon breakfast. Charlene and the redheaded man were nowhere to be seen. They were probably in Charlene's room upstairs, taking care of some mutual business.

"Do you have a room for rent?" he asked the bartender.

Henry nodded solemnly. "A dollar a day," he said as he studied an advertisement for a patented mange cure.

Slocum laid two of the dollars he had won off Hicks on the bar. "I'll be staying two," he said, picking up his rifle and saddlebags.

The barkeep reached under the counter and produced a brass skeleton key. "Room six," he mumbled.

Slocum looked over to the gambling table. Flanders and Sheriff Hicks sat there with a bottle between them, talking quietly. Hicks cast a long, curious glance at Slocum as the tall Georgian mounted the staircase, studying him as if he were a two-headed calf in some county fair sideshow. Then he grumbled something and poured himself another shot of rye whiskey.

Slocum paid Hicks no mind. He reached the second-floor landing and started around the balcony to where his room was located. As he passed room twelve he heard the squeaking of bedsprings and the low moans of passion.

Obviously Charlene's current business was swiftly reaching its climax, so to speak.

Before walking on to his room, Slocum paused for a moment and listened. It was clear to judge that the redheaded fellow's lustful groans were real enough. But to trained ears like Slocum's, Charlene's cries of delight seemed more theatrical than truthful. Slocum knew how a woman sounded when she was genuinely in the throes of pleasure and it sounded to him like Charlene was putting on quite a show.

As Slocum reached the door of his room and slipped the key into the slot, he told himself that he would give Charlene a try before leaving town. And when he did, there would be no deception between them. He'd do his best to strip the veneer of the saloon-savvy whore away and find the true passion of the woman that was hidden underneath.

6

After a long nap, Slocum rose fully rested, eager for more whiskey and gambling. He left his saddlebags and Winchester lying on the feather mattress of the big brass bed and stepped out on the landing, locking the door of his room behind him. An old German clock hanging on the wall at the head of the stairway chimed the hour of two.

Slocum was descending the stairs when he found his pathway blocked by the two men he had seen in the saloon earlier; the tall, lanky fellow with the oily black hair and the short man with the flaming red hair and freckles. From the way they stood at the foot of the stairs—casual, but with their hands close to their guns—Slocum knew that they were waiting for him and him alone.

"Mr. Smith?" asked the redheaded gunman.

"Yes?" replied Slocum flatly. His own Colt Navy was angled across his belly, scarcely a few inches away from his right hand.

"You're to come with us," said the tall fellow.

Slocum stopped five steps from the two and stood there, appraising them, wondering if they were as fast with those pistols as he was with his. "Who says?"

"The Judge, that's who," said the smaller of the two. "And I'd advise you to come along, if you don't want trouble. Believe me, the Judge ain't a man whose wrong side you want to get on."

37

Slocum considered the consequences of refusing the Judge's invitation, then figured that the odds were stacked against him. He was unfamiliar with Tyler's Crossing and its people, as well as the much feared Judge Burke and his hired guns turned lawmen. If Slocum wasn't careful, he could end up spending the next month in the town jail, or even worse if what Hinchburger and Charlene had told him was true.

The tall Georgian eased his hand away from his gun and relaxed. "All right, let's go see this judge."

As Slocum and the two deputies crossed the barroom, the Southerner could feel the eyes of the Plowman's patrons upon them. There were twice as many people in the saloon now, some drinking at the bar, while others sat at the tables talking and smoking. Flanders the gambler had a game of faro going. Charlene shared a table with a wet-eared kid who looked to be no more than sixteen. The whore now wore a dress of orange and black silk, along with a bright red feathered boa draped across her shapely shoulders. The boy's eyes were glued to Charlene's cleavage, while the saloon girl eyed Slocum and his escorts with interest. Slocum nodded to her quietly, then was ushered through the batwings by the Judge's men.

The town's main street was busier now than when Slocum had first arrived. It was filled with horse-drawn buggies and wagons, all churning up their fair share of dust as they traveled up and down the central thoroughfare. As they passed a number of businesses—a two-seat barbershop, a mercantile, and a gunsmith's shop—Slocum noticed a middle-aged man and his two young sons loading feed sacks into the back of a wagon. The man sported a black eye and several deep gashes on his face. The battered farmer cast a withering glance at the two deputies and spat venomously into the dust of the street, before turning back to the task at hand.

Soon they reached their destination—the two-story court-house of red brick and whitewashed oak. A few rough-looking fellows with low-slung Colts and brass badges lounged on the stone steps of the courthouse, telling jokes and chewing tobacco. Slocum pegged them as more of the Judge's cronies. They stopped their laughter as the three walked past, each man eyeing Slocum suspiciously, as if trying to determine whether he was a potential enemy or ally.

They entered the building and walked down a shadowy hallway to a staircase that led to the upper floor. As they began to climb the stairs, Slocum decided to ask a question. "Do you fellas have any idea why the Judge would want to see me? I'm just a stranger in town, you know."

The redhead shrugged. "Ain't none of our business really," he told Slocum. "But there's usually only three reasons why the Judge would want a man brought to him. First, he might want to hire you to do some sort of work for him. Secondly, he might not like the looks of you and want you to move on. Then there's the chance that he might want to see you for another reason. You're not a wanted man, are you, Mr. Smith?"

Slocum felt a jolt of adrenaline shoot through him. It was true that he did have a couple of wanted posters out on him, but they were years old and, he had hoped, faded from the attention of the law with time. Had someone in Tyler's Crossing recognized him as John Slocum and turned him in to the Judge? Luther Hicks maybe? Or perhaps Flanders or Henry the bartender? Slocum felt like drawing his Colt and attempting to escape the courthouse right then and there, but decided it might be best to wait and see what the purpose of his sudden visit to the Judge might be.

When they reached the second floor, they traveled down another corridor to a room at the far end. A tall, leathery man with pale blue eyes sat in a chair next to the office door, smoking a handrolled cigarette and holding a shotgun across his knees. There was a single point of interest that struck Slocum immediately. The guard's right hand was bandaged and a circle of blood had leaked through the cloth. Slocum knew instantly that the gauze hid a bullet wound that had been inflicted only a few hours ago.

The man studied Slocum with his icy eyes. "I reckon this must be Smith," he said. His voice was as flat and cold as his gaze was.

"That's right, Guthrie," said the redhead. "The Judge is expecting him."

Guthrie waved the shotgun's double barrels toward the doorway, motioning for them to go inside.

They entered the chambers of Judge Hamilton Burke. Slocum was impressed by the quality of the furnishings and the finery of the draperies and rug. It was clear to see that a lot had been spent decorating the room with the finest that money could buy. But it wasn't the room that Slocum had come there to see that afternoon. He ignored his surroundings and centered his attention on the man who sat behind the big maplewood desk at the far end of the room.

"Tipton, McGraw . . . you can go now," the Judge told his two men. When they had left, the most feared man in Tyler's Crossing beckoned to Slocum. "Come closer, Mr. Smith. Have a seat."

As Slocum approached the desk, he studied Judge Burke. The man was in his mid-sixties, frail and gray-haired, looking more like someone's elderly grandfather than a federal judge who had everyone in town shaking in their boots. There was one other thing that struck Slocum as being odd. The Judge was a cripple. He sat in a cane-backed wheelchair, an Indian blanket tucked neatly around his useless legs.

But the sense of danger that Slocum had sensed before arriving didn't diminish, even after seeing the Judge's feeble condition. Burke still possessed the glint of pure meanness in his bright eyes and carried a brace of silver-plated pepperbox pistols with mother-of-pearl handles in the pockets of his fancy vest. He was not a man to be trifled with, that was plain to see.

"Thanks for accepting my invitation, Mr. Smith," said the Judge with amused eyes.

"Looked to me like I didn't have much of a choice," Slocum replied.

Burke laughed humorlessly. "No, I suppose you didn't." He gestured toward an open box of cigars and a silver tray of liquor bottles that sat on one side of the desk. "Help yourself, Smith," he invited. "The cigars are the best from Cuba, straight from Havana. And the spirits are of the finest quality."

"I wouldn't think you'd accept any less than that," Slocum told him. He didn't hesitate in partaking of the Judge's private stock. He poured himself a shot glass of French cognac from a crystal decanter, then took one of the long cigars and bit the end off. As he settled into a leather wingback chair opposite the Judge's desk, Slocum took a match from his shirt pocket and lit the end of the Cuban cigar.

Judge Burke sat there and studied the drifter for a long moment, then spoke. "I suppose you're curious as to why I requested your presence here this afternoon, aren't you, Mr. Smith?"

Slocum decided to play it cool. "Maybe the least little bit," he said. He took a leisurely drag on the cigar, then chased the smoke down with a sip of the fancy French liquor.

That seemed to needle the Judge a little, but he tried not to let it show. "I just wanted to ask you a few questions, Mr. Smith. Like what sort of business you might have here in Tyler's Crossing? And how long do you intend to stay?"

"As to the business part, I really don't have any," said Slocum truthfully. "I'm just passing through on my way to Colorado. As to how long I'm staying, it won't be for long. Perhaps another day or so."

The Judge's liver-spotted hands squeezed idly at the padded armrests of his wheelchair as he leaned forward. "I don't know if you're aware of this, Mr. Smith, but anyone residing within my jurisdiction for a period of more than one day without gainful employment is considered a man without means of support and, therefore, subject to imprisonment in the county jail for a term of thirty days."

"Is that so?" asked Slocum. He couldn't say that he was surprised.

"Yes, Mr. Smith, that is so," said the Judge. "Now, tell me, have you sought employment since your arrival here in town?"

"No, sir, I can't say that I have."

Judge Burke eyed Slocum solemnly from beneath his heavy brows. "Very well, Mr. Smith. That leaves several options for you to mull over. You can either leave Tyler's Crossing by dawn tomorrow, you can stay and face a lengthy term in jail, or you can find a job. If you choose the latter, I may just be able to assist you."

"Oh?" asked Slocum. "Do you have some work for me?"

"Perhaps," said the Judge. "Last night, one of my deputies was severely wounded and it looks like he will have to forfeit his position. A man like yourself might fill that spot quite satisfactorily."

"May I ask what you mean by 'a man like myself'?" Slocum asked.

"A man proficient with firearms," said Burke. "I assume that you are. You carry that Colt Navy like you know how to use it and I've heard that you also carry a Winchester rifle."

"That's right," allowed Slocum. "But that doesn't make me a gun for hire."

"I'm not looking for hired guns," said the Judge. "Only deputies who know how to handle a gun and don't ask too many questions. Rest assured, I'm willing to pay top dollar for a man of your abilities. Twenty dollars a week to start."

"That's mighty tempting, Judge Burke," said Slocum. He emptied the shot glass in a single gulp, then ground the half-smoked stogie into the bottom of it. "But the thing is, I'm not deputy material. I'm just someone passing through. I want no ties to this town. I just want to rest up a mite, then go my way."

Judge Burke's eyes grew grim and his face as expressionless as stone. "Very well, Mr. Smith. I can't say that I didn't attempt to assist you. If your mind is made up, I will expect you to be clear of the town limits by daylight tomorrow. If you are still here, I will have no alternative than to jail you for breaking our statute."

"Don't worry," said Slocum, turning to leave. "I'll likely be in the next county before you've even risen from your bed in the morning."

"You see to that," said Burke. The Judge watched as Slocum headed for the office doorway. He spoke out before the man could leave, though. "One other thing, Mr. Smith."

Slocum turned and faced the Judge, annoyed. "And what would that be?"

"There was an incident at the farm of a man named George Kelly last night," said Burke. "Two men where badly wounded by an unknown gunman. Would you know anything about that, Mr. Smith?"

Slocum studied the Judge's eyes and detected the least hint of suspicion there. "No," he lied for his own sake. "I wouldn't."

"Then good day to you, sir," said Hamilton Burke, dismissing him with a wave of his bony hand. "And good riddance."

Slocum left the Judge's chamber and stepped out into the hallway. As he started down the corridor, he passed Guthrie, Timpton, and McGraw. The men watched him as he headed for the stairway. Slocum half expected them to follow, but they didn't. Obviously, they had done what the Judge had instructed them to do. Slocum was no concern of theirs now.

And, hopefully, they would no longer be any concern of his either.

7

After leaving Hamilton Burke's office at the Tyler's Crossing courthouse, Slocum returned to the Plowman Saloon. He felt relieved that he had escaped his appointment with the Judge with his freedom intact, but he also felt more than a little peeved that he had been given an ultimatum: join up with Burke's bogus deputies or suffer incarceration. Of course, it really made no difference to Slocum. He would be more than happy to continue on his way. The Kansas town had given him nothing but trouble since he first arrived.

Upon entering the saloon at a little before three o'clock, Slocum stepped up to the bar, bought a bottle from Henry, then found an empty table next to the staircase. He sat there, drinking and smoking, for a while, trying to drive the Kellys and their struggle against the Judge and his nightriders from his thoughts. It was difficult for him to do so. Time and time again, Prissy kept coming to mind: her lovely eyes and smile, as well as the intimacy they had shared in the cramped confines of the hayloft. He kept telling himself that he owed the woman and her father nothing, that they meant nothing to him, and that it would be best to simply ride off and forget them. But that was easier said than done.

Perhaps it had something to do with the Judge himself. Slocum certainly had no great love for judges. It was a damned judge who had given Slocum reason to leave his farm in Georgia and seek exile in the vast wilderness of the West. The carpetbagger had intended to take Slocum's land away from him, but had only taken a fatal slug from the Georgian's Navy revolver instead. A warrant for Slocum had been issued, but so far he had escaped the wrath of the federal government.

That was why it would be in his best interest to simply ride away from Tyler's Crossing and leave the Judge's dishonorable intentions for George Kelly and the other farmers to worry about. But, again, there was another part of the tall Southerner who would like nothing more than to see Hamilton Burke fail at his crooked plan . . . and fail severely.

As the autumn sunset bled away into the cool darkness of evening, Slocum joined Flanders at the gambling table for several games of blackjack. As the night drew on, the crowd began to thin out. Soon the only ones in the saloon were Slocum and the gambler, Charlene and a potential john, and Luther Hicks and six of his deputies, who kept to themselves at a corner table, drinking and talking quietly.

A little after ten, the batwing doors swung open and the gaunt, pale-eyed man named Guthrie walked in. Slocum watched from where he sat as Guthrie crossed the room to Hicks's table. The two men exchanged low words, then Hicks dug his pocket watch from his vest and flipped the ornate lid. He studied the time and nodded. Then he and the others left their table and followed Guthrie outside.

At first, Slocum intended to keep his seat at the gambling table, figuring that what Luther Hicks and the others were up to was none of his business. Then his curiosity got the better of him. Whatever they were up to at that late hour, it was certainly no good. Slocum sighed heavily, bowed out of the game, and rose. He crossed the saloon, then pushed through the doorway into the night. He breathed in the cool air deeply. The stench of tobacco smoke, liquor, and the sweat of men was becoming too thick between the walls of the Plowman Saloon. The clarity and openness of the Kansas night was much less claustrophobic to a man like John Slocum.

He took one last drag from his cigarette, then tossed it to the dusty boards of the sidewalk and ground the butt beneath the heel of his boot. Slocum stepped quickly away from the saloon doorway, on the chance that Hicks or one of his men might see his silhouette against the inner light. But the group—which had increased to eleven in number since reaching the street—paid him no mind. They continued on their way, talking quietly as they headed toward the eastern end of town.

Toward the livery stable.

Slocum clung to the shadows, following silently. When Hicks and his men reached their destination, Slocum ducked into an alleyway and watched as they entered the livery barn. He waited for nearly ten minutes, hearing and seeing nothing, before the band appeared once again. This time they emerged from the rear corral of the livery, dressed completely in black from head to toe, and riding mounts as black as the unlit shaft of a coal mine.

Quietly, so as not to draw attention, they walked their horses down the main street of Tyler's Crossing. Then, when they reached the western limits of the little town, they spurred their mounts forward. The moonless night swallowed the band of nightriders instantly.

As the thunderous drumming of shod hooves diminished into the distance, Slocum made up his mind. He had to see what they were up to. He swiftly crossed the street and stepped into the livery stable.

Slocum closed the door behind him and listened. He could hear the loud snoring of the liveryman in an adjoining room. Apparently, Hicks and the others had crept past Hinchburger without the blacksmith being any the wiser. Slocum did the same. He searched the stable until he found the stall that housed his own spotted gelding. Then he quietly saddled the horse and led it silently from the stock barn.

The tall Georgian climbed into the saddle and reined the gelding westward. He thought for a moment more, wondering if his actions were sensible or downright foolhardy. Then he recalled the scarred flesh of George Kelly's aged back and the nightrider's dark whip of braided rawhide, and he knew he must proceed.

He spurred the gelding, sending it galloping down the street and out of town . . . in the general direction that Hicks and the band of ebony riders had headed in.

At first, Slocum was certain that he had lost them. The dust of the trail had settled and he could hear no sound, not the pounding of hooves or the quiet snorting of horses that had been ridden too hard. There was only the silence of the night and the soft sounds of his own gelding beneath him.

He continued westward, aware that he had been riding for nearly half an hour now. On both sides of the trail stood tall stands of corn. The stalks stood like solemn sentries, swaying to and fro in a stiff gale that rolled across the Kansas plains from the north.

Slocum was considering giving up the pursuit and returning to town when the distinctive crack of a gunshot rang from less than a quarter mile ahead.

He urged his gelding onward. As he approached the low, dark buildings of a modest farmstead, he slowed the horse and reined it to a halt. Slocum leapt from the saddle, tethered the animal to a fence post, then slipped over strands of barbed wire into the close-grown rows of a vast cornfield. The brittle rustle of the windblown leaves masked Slocum's footsteps as he made his way through the crop and stopped a few feet from the western perimeter. There, he crouched in the concealment of the corn, watching the dirt yard of a crudely built sod house and what was taking place there.

The nightriders stood in a half circle around a family of Negroes. A woman in her thirties cowered in the doorway of the house, gathering her three children close to her. Her husband, a strapping young man who appeared as big as a bull and nearly as strong, was on his knees, struggling as two of Hicks's men tied his hands behind his back. The black man spat contemptuously into the masked face of one of the riders, eliciting his wrath. Hatefully, the nightrider struck out with the barrel of his pistol, splitting the Negro's scalp and drawing a trickle of blood. Slocum recognized the revolver as being a Colt Dragoon and instantly knew that the attacker was none other than Luther Hicks.

"Best get that sass outta you right now, Jackson," demanded Hicks. "If there's something I can't stand, it's a nigger who thinks he's the equal of a white man."

Slocum couldn't believe it, but it sounded as if the black man was laughing. "Ha!" grated the farmer named Jackson. "It'll be a cold day in hell when the likes of you is the equal of me! Why you ain't higher than maggots in mule shit, as far as I'm concerned!"

"Just don't learn, do you, nigger?" questioned Hicks. Before the man could answer, the leader of the nightriders reared back and delivered a savage kick to the man's groin. Jackson doubled over, gagging beneath the sheer agony of the blow.

One of the nightriders walked his mount forward . . . a tall man with a coil of knotted leather in his left hand. "Let me have a go at him, boss," echoed the voice of Guthrie. "He'll behave when he gets a taste of the whip."

"No," said Hicks, shaking his head. "He's had the whip too many times already and hasn't learned a damned thing. I reckon his kind fears only one kind of teaching." He turned toward one of the riders. "Take that rope and sling it over the limb of that oak over yonder."

The wife of the black farmer screamed and ran forward, her hands outstretched. "No, mister! Please, don't hang my poor Elias. He's been meaning to go into town and sign them papers you mentioned before, but he's been busy. Give him another chance. Please, just one more."

The undisguised hatred that blazed in the black man's eyes told Hicks otherwise. "Don't give me that, woman. It's clear to see he has no intention of being a good darkie and doing as he's been told. Now he'll have to suffer for his disobedience." He motioned for several of his men to dismount. "Hang the black bastard!"

It took six of the nightriders to drag the big Negro to the towering oak tree that grew next to the sod house. Finally, after much wrestling, they dragged him beneath the most sturdy of the oak's limbs. A length of hemp dangled over the bough and a hangman's noose awaited at the end. The rope was looped over Elias Jackson's broad neck and tightened. Then the other end of the rope was tied securely to the saddle horn of a nightrider's horse.

In the corn rows, Slocum watched as the horse backed away, leaving the lynch rope taut. Slocum could stand to watch no longer. He knew the dread that settled in a man's stomach when facing the threat of hanging. Slocum himself had felt the itchy tightness of the rope around his own neck several times, although fate had always allowed his escape. However, it didn't appear that the Grim Reaper would be quite so merciful with Elias Jackson. Slowly the Negro began to rise from his knees under no effort of his own. The noose was rising skyward, taking the black farmer with it.

Slocum slipped the thong off his Colt Navy and drew it from its holster. He stood up amid the corn stalks, ready to step out of his concealment and begin firing. He knew that bucking such odds was foolish, but he couldn't allow himself to simply hide there in the cornfield while this proud man strangled to death in front of the eyes of his family.

Slocum was thumbing back the hammer of his pistol when Luther Hicks laughed loudly and signaled to the rider who handled the rope. The nightrider nodded and slipped the knot loose from his saddle horn. The length of oiled hemp lost its tightness, sending Jackson crashing back into the dusty earth. The other nightriders joined Hicks's laughter as the Negro rolled over and gasped deeply, attempting to regain his lost breath.

Hicks walked over and knelt next to the farmer. He pressed the muzzle of the Dragoon squarely between the man's eyes. "Now you listen up, Jackson. You've got one more chance to do the right thing . . . just one more, do you understand? If you don't show up at the courthouse with deed in hand by sundown tomorrow, we'll be back. And next time, your appointment with the rope won't be cut short."

Elias Jackson said nothing. He simply lay there, staring at the earth beneath him and breathing in great gulps of precious air.

"And you won't be the only one to suffer, nigger," promised Guthrie from his horse. "Your dying won't be near as bad as what your woman and young'uns will endure. Theirs will be much slower and painful, I promise you that."

Even from where Slocum stood, he could see that the last threat served its intended effect. All the tension drained from Jackson's dark muscles, as if his rage had abruptly burned out. The threat of harm to his loved ones seemed to break his spirit completely.

"Come on, boys," said Hicks, sliding his .44 back into its holster. "Let's let Jackson chew on that for a while. I'm sure he's seen the light now."

"We'll see about that," grumbled Guthrie. His good hand gripped the haft of the bullwhip tightly, as if yearning to lay leather to the black man's heaving back.

Slocum watched as one of the nightriders walked over and cut the farmer's bonds, then mounted his horse as the others did. They watched as Jackson's wife and children ran to him, weeping fearfully. Some laughed, while others simply gloated in silence.

"Remember, Jackson," said Hicks as he reined his stallion toward the trail. "Sundown tomorrow and no later."

Then he and the others rode swiftly back in the direction of town.

For several moments Slocum stood in the shadows of the cornfield, watching as the black family recovered from the nocturnal assault that had been visited upon them. Jackson's wife attempted to help her injured husband to his feet, but failed at her first few attempts. Slocum considered emerging from the field and assisting her, but thought better of it. Elias Jackson had suffered enough humiliation that night. Slocum's sudden appearance out of nowhere would more than likely make matters worse.

He watched as Jackson finally regained his feet under his own power, then hobbled back to the sod house, his family gathered around him. Then the simple wooden door closed behind them, leaving the dwelling dark and silent.

Slocum reholstered his Colt and picked his way back through the cornfield. Moments later he emerged from the rows and found his horse waiting where it had been tethered. Luckily, the nightriders had ridden past it totally unaware, thanks to the absence of a moon that night.

Slocum untied his gelding, then climbed into the saddle. As he turned toward Tyler's Crossing and started back to town, an uneasiness filled him. What Slocum had seen at the Jackson farm that night had sickened him. He knew then that Luther Hicks and his band of cutthroats were men to be avoided, at any cost.

And, more and more, Slocum was reaching the conclusion that it would be in his best interest to do just that.

8

It was well past midnight when Slocum made it back to Tyler's Crossing. He spirited his spotted gelding back into its stall in Hinchburger's stable, then made his way inconspicuously back to the Plowman Saloon. The crowd in the saloon was still large, even at that late hour, and all were concerned with their individual vices. They would have probably never noticed Slocum's entrance, but he decided not to take any chances. He avoided the direct path across the rowdy barroom, instead making his way to a flight of stairs at the western side of the two-story building.

Slocum climbed the staircase and opened a door leading to the inner balcony. As he stepped inside and walked around the upper landing, he looked down at the smoky saloon below. Flanders the gambler was closing up shop for the evening, putting away his chips and cards, and tugging on his black frock coat. Henry was wiping down the long walnut bar, getting ready to hustle out his drunken clientele and call it a night himself. Slocum, too, felt the weariness of that day's events begin to pull at him like a heavy weight. All he wanted now was to undress and settle into the feather bed of the room he had rented for that night.

He withdrew the brass key from his vest pocket and turned it in the lock. The room was pitch-dark. As he reached for the coal-oil lamp on the decorative table next to the door, Slocum heard the slightest creak of the bedsprings across the room from him. In an instant, he had the Colt Navy drawn and cocked.

"Who's there?" he demanded.

A woman giggled softly. "About time you showed up. That was quite an evening's stroll you took. Seems like I've been waiting up here half the night."

Slocum breathed in deeply, drawing in a peculiar odor. He recognized it immediately as the scent of fancy French perfume. He had smelled that particular aroma before and knew exactly who it belonged to.

"Charlene?" he asked, returning his gun to its holster and fumbling for a sulfur match. "What are you doing here?"

"You might say I'm paying a social call," said the woman in a low, husky voice. "Fact is, I got tired of waiting for you to come to me, so I decided to come to you instead."

Slocum raised the lamp's chimney and lit the wick. A warm yellow glow dispelled the darkness, revealing the upstairs room and Slocum's unexpected visitor rather clearly.

Charlene's fancy dress of bright silk, black lace, and colored ostrich plumes lay folded over the back of a chair across the room, along with her undergarments, sheer black stockings, and high-button shoes. The woman herself waited in the feather bed. Slocum felt his exhaustion vanish as he closed the door and eyed the buxom saloon girl. Charlene was naked, the lower half of her body concealed by the bed linen. The sheet was draped enticingly across the generous swell of her breasts. Brown nipples peeked from over the very edge of the blanket, like broad copper coins there for the taking.

Slocum felt himself stir below the belt buckle. "Don't think that I haven't felt the need to partake of your services, Charlene," he told the woman as he removed his gunbelt and hung it over a corner post of the big brass bed. "Truth of the matter is, I was just waiting for the urge to hit me."

Charlene arched one of her long legs and, with her foot, pulled the rest of the sheet away. Her lithe body with its creamy skin, pert breasts, and downy thatch of golden hair was suddenly revealed in the lamplight. "So, this urge of yours . . . has it hit you yet?"

Slocum nodded and walked to the bed. "It has," he told her.

Charlene reached up and pulled the tall Georgian onto the bed next to her. Slocum captured the woman's mouth with his own. He felt his britches grow tighter at the crotch as Charlene's hands worked at him. Soon, she had performed her task. Slocum's clothing lay in a pile on the floor and the drifter was as naked as she was.

"Yes," Charlene hissed in his ear as she grabbed his manhood, wrapping her long fingers around its thickness. "I knew it. I knew you would be big." She stroked at him, increasing his length and hardness.

Slocum groaned, relishing the feel of her hand on his cock. He lowered his head and took the tip of a breast into his mouth. He sucked lightly, then harder. Charlene's nipple stiffened between his lips. The action had the intended effect. Charlene moaned softly, begging for him to do the same to her other tit. He obliged her, heightening her arousal even more.

"Take me, John," pleaded Charlene. "Put it in me now!"

Slocum could tell by the trembling of her body and the heat in her lovely violet-blue eyes that the passion Charlene exhibited was not an act. No, it was truly genuine. Satisfied, Slocum positioned himself over the writhing female and guided himself toward the wetness between her legs.

Charlene squealed as Slocum buried himself in, up to the hilt. The Georgian was still for a moment, enjoying the fleshy warmth that engulfed him. Then he began to stroke. His rhythm was slow at first, then increased in tempo. Charlene moaned sultrily, her full lips pursed. She began to buck her hips up to meet him, as if unable to wait another second for the thrust of his manly spear.

After a few minutes, Charlene looked up boldly into Slocum's lustful eyes. "I want to do it different," she whispered. "Let me show you."

Slocum withdrew from her and allowed her to take the reins for a moment. The long-legged blonde turned over, positioning herself atop the mattress on her hands and knees. "Do me like this," she asked. "Hurry!"

Slocum wasted no time. He knelt on the bed and, grabbing her firm ass in his tanned hands, sank into her from behind. The portal of her sex grasped him like a wet fist as her thighs clenched and he nearly lost it. He regained control, however, and continued his measured stroking.

The minutes passed. The sweat of raw passion bathed them both, serving as a natural lubricant. Slocum leaned over Charlene's smooth back, tonguing the nape of her neck and reaching beneath her body, squeezing and kneading her dangling breasts. Soon, Charlene began to shudder and cry out. Her shout rose in pitch and her inner muscles clamped down on him. Slocum could hold out no longer. He groaned and thrust hard as he shot his load. Eventually, Charlene's cries of ecstasy faded into soft coos of contentment.

As Slocum rolled over and Charlene settled onto the mattress next to him, the dark-haired Georgian pushed a sprig of fallen hair from the woman's perspiring face. "So, what do I owe you?" he asked with a sly grin.

"Are you kidding?" said Charlene with a laugh. "After that, I should be paying you!"

They lay there together for a while, allowing themselves to cool down and relax a bit. Slocum was delighted when Charlene reached down next to the bed and brought out a bottle of the saloon's best whiskey. She had neglected to bring glasses, so Slocum pulled the cork with his teeth and they passed the liquor back and forth.

"I saw the Judge's men come for you this afternoon," Charlene finally said. "Did you have some business with that crippled old coot?"

"Maybe he thought so," Slocum told her, "but I didn't."

"It's best that you stand clear of Burke," she advised. "He's like a dose of bad medicine with a little arsenic thrown in for good measure."

Slocum didn't tell her about the ultimatum he had been given. He figured it would be easier to simply ride away without having to explain himself. "What can you tell me about this Judge Burke?" he asked the blonde.

Charlene shrugged her shapely shoulders. "Not very much. He was assigned to Tyler's Crossing about three years ago by the government, on account there's been a lot of cattle rustling and Indian trouble down around the Oklahoma border. I heard he was a Northern lawyer before the war and a carpetbagging judge afterward. Whatever part of the South he was in charge of, I'm sure they purely despised the bastard. Some Johnny Reb ambushed him on a country road, shot him in the back, and crippled him for life. But apparently that only made him meaner. Ever since he was assigned to Tyler's Crossing, the Judge has been passing his own laws and fining folks for outrageous things like parking their wagons on the wrong side of the street or some such silly crime. Lately, he's been pushing his authority too far. He's started raising the land taxes on the farmers hereabouts and expecting them to pay when they can't possibly raise the money. And there's this ugly business with the nightriders harassing them in the dead of night. Most of the farmers are scared to talk about what's been happening, but everyone is certain it has a connection to the Judge and his shady dealings."

"Then what you're saying is that he's a man to be avoided," said Slocum.

"That's right," replied Charlene. The whore thought to herself for a moment, then smiled wickedly. "Although it would be nice to see someone stand up to Burke for a change. Maybe show him that he isn't lord and master over us all."

Slocum said little after that. Conversation between him and the blonde faded as Charlene gradually drifted off to sleep. Slocum lay there for a while, letting the exhaustion of fornication and the intoxicating effects of the liquor lull him, too, into slumber.

Before sleep claimed him, however, John Slocum thought long and hard about Judge Hamilton Burke and the ultimatum the man had given him. Slocum had been given a similar warning once before, also by a judge. A land-coveting judge whose name Slocum didn't even know. The man had used the law in order to force Slocum from his own property, intending to use it for his own selfish gains. But when the judge and a henchman returned later, they found not a common dirt farmer, but a seasoned gunman wearing twin Colt Navies. They had misjudged Slocum and had paid for their ignorance with their lives.

But this situation was different, Slocum told himself as he fell asleep. He had no such stake in Tyler's Crossing . . . no ties of land or heritage to make this fight his own. No, he knew that this conflict belonged to others. It would be best if he just rode away from this little farming town and left the notorious Judge Burke and his band of clandestine nightriders for folks like George Kelly and Elias Jackson to deal with.

9

At dawn, Slocum rose, dressed quietly, and gathered up his gear. He stared down at Charlene, who slept with the innocence of a child on the opposite side of the brass bed. He cherished the memory of the passion they had shared the night before, then pushed it out of his mind. He placed a couple of gold pieces on the pillow next to her, then let himself out of the room.

Slocum left through the side door and descended the outer stairway to the alley below. The main street was empty, but the drifter saw lights in several windows and smelled the tangy aroma of woodsmoke in the early morning air. He slung his saddlebags over his shoulder and, rifle in hand, walked across the street to the livery stable.

Hinchburger was already up and setting up shop in the lean-to outside. He had already stoked the fire of his smithy and had a pot of coffee and a pan of biscuits cooking over the flames. "Morning," greeted the liveryman. He eyed Slocum curiously, studying the gear and Winchester. "You heading out already?"

"That's the idea I woke up with," Slocum simply said.

"I heard that the Judge called you to the courthouse for a talk," said Hinchburger. "I reckon it concerned that stupid law of his. The one about finding work or else moving on."

Slocum nodded. "You reckoned right."

Hinchburger scratched his wooly beard. "If you want to stay on for a while longer, I could probably find some chores for you to do here around the livery."

"Much obliged for the offer," Slocum said sincerely. "But this town hasn't made that much of an impression on me. I reckon I'll ride on before me and that judge ends up locking horns."

Hinchburger turned back to check on his breakfast. "Yeah, I understand. Lot of bad going on here in town. No need to involve yourself with it."

As Slocum passed the lean-to and walked on to the big doors of the stock barn, he strangely felt like a coward in the blacksmith's eyes. He knew that it was probably his imagination, but he couldn't help but think it just the same.

Slocum walked to the stall that held his gelding. The horse smelled its master and snorted softly. Slocum stepped into the stall and ran a comforting hand along the animal's neck. Hinchburger had taken good care of the horse. The gelding had been fed its fill of oats and its spotted coat had been brushed and groomed. As Slocum left the animal and approached the adjoining wall, he found that his saddle had been cleaned and oiled also. It was plain to see that Hinchburger was a man who put a little extra effort into the work he did for other folks.

The dark-haired Southerner had his fists around the saddle, ready to pitch it onto the gelding's back and secure it tightly, when he stopped in his tracks. In the gloom of the stable, Slocum could picture the Judge's grizzled features grinning at him in triumph. If Slocum picked up and left at that moment, Burke would have accomplished what he set out to do the previous afternoon . . . run off an undesirable saddle tramp with the threat of jail, like he had probably done countless times before.

At that moment, standing there in the stable on the verge of leaving, Slocum thought about the Judge and his illegal crusade for the hard-earned money of defenseless farmers. Slocum had been a farmer once himself and, in spite of himself, felt a kindredship toward those who tilled the earth from dawn to dusk. If Slocum left now, he would leave with the guilt of knowing that Kelly and the others would more than likely pay with the cost of their livelihood . . . and perhaps even their lives before it was all over and done with.

Slocum released his saddle, letting it settle back to its place on top of the wall. "I ain't gonna do it," he rasped beneath his breath. "I ain't gonna let that crippled son of a bitch railroad me."

He took his saddlebags and rifle, and went back outside.

Hinchburger was surprised. "I thought you'd be saddled by now."

Slocum eyed the coffee and biscuits hungrily. "How much would you charge a man for some breakfast?"

The liveryman seemed eager for company. "Help yourself," insisted Hinchburger. As they split up the food and coffee, the big man appraised Slocum. "So, did you have a change of heart?"

Slocum sipped on a mug of coffee. It was just like he liked it: jet-black and as hot as hellfire. "You might say that."

"And that job I offered?"

"I reckon I'll have to pass on that one," he told the man. "Besides, I've already been offered work, probably at better wages than you're willing to offer me."

Hinchburger's face darkened a degree. "You mean doing dirty work for the Judge, don't you?"

Slocum studied the brawny blacksmith for a long moment and figured him to be a fairly honest man. However, he could be wrong and Hinchburger might be one of the Judge's hired spies that Charlene had told him about. He remembered the first place Luther Hicks and his men had gone before setting off on their last ride. "What about you?" he asked the man, testing him for the right answer. "You said that the Judge was one of your customers."

"I just keep some horses for the man, that's all," Hinchburger said defensively. "Just a dozen black stallions in the corral out back."

"Twelve black horses for twelve men dressed in black?"

Hinchburger's face grew red with shame. "I don't ask no questions, mister. If I did, I'd likely be out of business . . . or worse."

Slocum could tell that Hinchburger detested the pompous judge as much as anyone else in town, maybe even more. And he felt like the man could be trusted, too. At least he hoped so.

"What do you know about this business the Judge is running on the farmers hereabouts?" he asked the man. "Exactly what is he trying to do?"

Hinchburger cast a wary glance along the deserted street, then lowered his voice. "Well, at first I figured the Judge was aiming to take their land away from them. You know, do like those thieving carpetbaggers did down South and claim that the landowners were owing on back taxes, then confiscate their property. But he's had the chance to do that and he ain't done it yet. I think what he's really doing is running some sort of shady protection racket. I hail from New York City myself, and there was a lot of that going on with the shopkeepers up there, usually from the Irish and the Italians. They'd bust up their stores, then charge them to keep it from happening again."

"So you think the Judge is trying to milk money from the farmers to assure that the nightriders don't make a sudden appearance in the middle of the night?" Slocum asked.

"That's what I believe to be so," Hinchburger said. "I've talked to a few of the farmers and they say the Judge is trying to get them to sign over a percentage of their land to him."

Slocum began to see what Hinchburger was getting at. The Judge had abandoned the blatant injustices common to his carpetbagging past and was running some sort of secretive extortion racket. "What about getting word to a U.S. marshal about what's been going on? Maybe they could impeach the bastard and boot him out of office."

"Don't think that some folks haven't considered doing just that," said the liveryman. "But there's a couple of important things to consider. Burke controls both the mail and the telegraph here in Tyler's Crossing. He has the postmaster and the head of the telegraph office in his hip pocket. If anyone was to send such a damning letter or wire to the marshal's office in Fort Atkinson, Hicks and that mangy bunch would be on them quicker than a hound on a June bug."

"You're probably right," agreed Slocum.

Suddenly Hinchburger's eyes grew suspicious. "But, hell, why am I telling you all this? You're actually thinking about joining up with the Judge's gang!"

"Not for the reason you think," assured the tall Georgian. "You see, I've got a low tolerance for high-handed judges who twist the law to their own liking."

A grin began to split Hinchburger's bearded face. "If you're intending to do what I think you are, you could end up in a mess of trouble. If Hicks and the others discovered that there was a spy in their midst, they'd likely skin you alive and nail your hide to the courthouse wall."

"More than likely," said Slocum. "But I don't aim to be found out that easily. All I want to do is learn exactly what's going on, maybe see if there's something we can do to put a stop to the Judge and his nightriders."

"I'm willing to do my part," promised the blacksmith. "I hear about all the gossip in town, the line of work I'm in. If the Judge gets wind of what your true intentions are, I oughtta be able to warn you before it's too late."

"That's what I'm depending on," said Slocum.

They grew quiet as they finished up the breakfast of biscuits and coffee. Then Hinchburger spoke up. "Oh, there's one other thing you ought to know. In the case of one farmer, the Judge is aiming to get his grubby hands on more than mere money. The fellow is named Kelly and the Judge has had his eye on the old man's daughter ever since he took office here in Tyler's Crossing. I don't know why the Judge wants her . . . he sure as hell can't do anything, what with his lower half pretty much dead and shriveled. Maybe he just wants Prissy Kelly for the sake of having her. She is the prettiest woman in these parts, except for maybe Charlene over at the saloon."

Slocum said nothing about his brief stay at the Kelly farm or his roll in the hay with Prissy. As he emptied the dregs of his coffee back into the pot, Slocum couldn't deny that Hamilton Burke's intentions toward Prissy Kelly bothered him somewhat. Not because he had any lasting feelings for the girl—a drifter such as Slocum couldn't hope to build a normal life or raise a decent family, not with the sort of past he had come from. But the very thought of sweet Prissy becoming an innocent victim during the course of Burke's villainous scheme only increased his anger and resentment toward the elderly man.

Slocum knew then that he would do what it took to bring the Judge down. And that he would relish every moment of his eventual defeat.

10

When Slocum entered the Tyler's Crossing courthouse that morning, he found the front steps devoid of the gathering he had encountered the previous day. None of the bogus deputies congregated there at that early hour. The only one Slocum came across was an old man who spent his time whittling a stick of soft pine while his toothless jaws worked on half a plug of chewing tobacco.

He entered the building and climbed the stairs to the second floor. There he found Guthrie sitting in the same spot he had occupied yesterday afternoon. The lanky, light-eyed man still held the scattergun across his lap, but obviously last night's trip to the Jackson farm and back had paid its toll on him. He was reared back in his chair, dozing soundly.

Slocum was almost to the door of the Judge's office when Guthrie awoke with a start. He lifted the twelve-gauge and centered its double barrels on Slocum's chest. "Where the hell do you think you're going?" he growled.

"I want to talk to Burke," the Georgian told him flatly.

Guthrie studied Slocum distastefully. "The Judge didn't say anything to me about having a meeting with·you this morning."

"That's because it wasn't exactly on his schedule," said Slocum. "Just the same, I'd like to see him." The tall Southerner felt his temper begin to rise. He remembered the eagerness Guthrie had shown toward taking the whip to

George Kelly. Next to Luther Hicks, Guthrie was Slocum's least favorite of the Judge's men.

Guthrie glared at Slocum for a tense moment, then shifted his gaze to the Colt Navy in its crossdraw holster. The thumb of Slocum's right hand was hooked in his gunbelt, scarcely two inches from the curved butt of the six-shooter. Guthrie stared at the pistol for a moment, then swallowed dryly. "I'll go ask him," he said, lowering his shotgun and leaving his chair. A moment later he had stepped through the office door, closing it behind him.

Away from Guthrie's scrutiny, Slocum released a breath of relief. If there was one thing that put him on edge, it was having the muzzle of a gun trained on him, especially one as destructive as a twelve-gauge. He waited in the hallway only a few seconds before Guthrie returned, an expression of disgust on his ugly face.

"Go on in," he said, returning to his chair. "He's waiting for you."

Slocum stepped into the office to find Hamilton Burke behind his huge desk as usual. The Judge sat in his wheelchair, sipping coffee from a china cup. On the desk was a serving set of sterling silver that probably cost more than most men earned during an entire year of back-breaking work.

"Ah, Mr. Smith," said the Judge, watching Slocum as he entered the room. His eyes held their usual stern expression, but the drifter could detect a definite hint of underlying satisfaction there also. "To what do I owe this unexpected visit?"

"I reckon you probably know that," said Slocum. "I've decided to stay in town awhile longer, and if it's necessary for me to take a job in order to stay, I figure I might as well make some money."

Burke smiled. "So you've decided to accept my offer. Excellent. I can always use a man of your abilities."

"How do you know I'm what you think I am?" asked Slocum. "I could be some loser who doesn't know one end of a gun from the other."

"I've dealt with your kind numerous times during my career as a judge, Smith," said Burke. "I'm sure that you're satisfactorily proficient with that .36 revolver. Just the same, you're right. I could very well be mistaken. That's why—if you're willing to hire on—I'll have Sheriff Hicks test your shooting skills thoroughly before you are placed on the payroll. Do you have any objections to that?"

"No, sir," said Slocum. In fact, he was rather glad to have the chance to be put to the test. Maybe in the process, he would be able to find out if Luther Hicks was still as good a hand with that Dragoon as he had been during their mutual stint in the Confederacy. It would be good to know how formidable an adversary Hicks might be, if things were to go suddenly wrong.

"Good," said the Judge. "You'll be paid twenty dollars a week in gold coin and your room and board will be provided at the Plowman. Frivolities such as liquor and women will be paid out of your own pocket. Just make sure that neither one affects your ability to do your job. One other thing. I trust that you have no objections to being on call, any hour of the night or day?"

"Sounds fine to me," said Slocum, though he gave no evidence that he even knew what his duties as one of the Judge's deputies might consist of.

"Very well," said Judge Burke. "Report to Hicks and let him know that you're joining up. He'll know what to do. You'll likely find him at the saloon." The Judge nailed Slocum with a grim look. "There's one thing more you must remember, Smith. Hicks is your superior. No matter what he wants you to do, you're to obey his orders. No matter how distasteful you might consider them to be."

"I understand," said Slocum. As the Judge turned his attention back to to his morning coffee, Slocum took his leave, putting the meeting to an end.

As he closed the door behind him, he found Guthrie glaring at him from his chair. Obviously, he had heard most of what had been said in the adjoining room.

"The Judge just made a big mistake, if you ask me," said Guthrie. "Just remember this, Smith. Watch your back. If you slip up even once, me and the boys won't think very kindly of it. You could end up sleeping in a pine box with six feet of earth as a blanket."

Slocum turned the blatant threat over in his mind and knew that Guthrie wasn't lying. He was walking a thin line and he knew it. He tried not to let his anger show, smiling thinly instead. "Bold talk for a man with a hole in his hand."

Guthrie flexed his bandaged hand. "It ain't as bad as it looks," he said coldly. "Besides, I'm fair enough aim with either hand . . . be it with a pistol or anything else."

Slocum said nothing else. He turned and headed back down the hallway before their hostile bantering grew into something much more dangerous. He descended the stairway and stepped out into the bright Kansas sun. Satisfied that the first step of his plan had been completed without suspicion, Slocum set off down main street to find Luther Hicks.

"Okay, Smith," said Hicks. "Let's see what you can do with that Colt pistol of yours." He set the last of six whiskey bottles on the top of a weathered fencerow and stepped out of harm's way.

Slocum stood a good thirty feet away, eyeing the half-dozen bottles as if they were made of flesh and blood and intending to gun him down. He took the Colt Navy from its holster, checked the loads, then returned it to its rightful place. He waited until Hicks had walked over to a dilapidated outhouse. The big Missourian leaned with his broad back to the wall, puffing on a noxious cigar as he appraised the newly hired deputy's stance and ease of balance.

The tall Georgian flexed his right hand and let it hover over the jutting curve of the revolver's handle. Then, swiftly, he shucked it from the holster and leveled it at arm's length. He didn't fire it like a lot of the trick shooters that were so plentiful in carnivals and traveling shows those days. No hip-shooting or fanning, just the quick and steady thumbing of the hammer and the smooth pull of the hair trigger immediately afterward. The octagon barrel of the .36 bucked with flame and burnt powder, and five seconds later all six bottles were gone, evaporated into spinning shards of glass by six well-placed shots.

After the report of Slocum's gun had died, Hicks took a pull on his cigar and let the smoke roll from the pits of his nostrils. He nodded approvingly. "Good," he said. "Pretty damn good."

Slocum said nothing in reply. As he disengaged the Colt's cylinder and, taking a preloaded spare from his vest pocket, slid it into place, the drifter recalled the events that took place directly after his departure from the Tyler's Crossing courthouse. He had found Sheriff Hicks precisely where the Judge had expected him to be . . . spending his morning at the Plowman Saloon, sharing a bottle and a deck of cards with Flanders the gambler. When Slocum had informed Burke's right-hand man of his hiring, Hicks hadn't seemed the least bit surprised. In fact, he actually seemed to expect the news. Together, they had gone to the livery, saddled their horses, and ridden several miles south of town, crossing a barren stretch of scrubby wilderness that had likely bore acre upon acre of wheat and barley sometime in the past. After an hour's ride, they arrived at an abandoned farmstead. It consisted of nothing more than a ramshackle house, two or three outbuildings, and a barn with a collapsed roof. There, he and Hicks had begun the task of testing Slocum's proficiency with firearms.

As Slocum finished priming his pistol and returned it to its holster, he eyed the big Dragoon lashed to Hick's right hip. "I reckon you can handle that hogleg .44 just as well?" he asked, his statement more of a challenge than a question.

Hicks grinned, showing off crooked rows of tobacco-stained teeth. "That's right," he said, leaving the shade of the privy with a swagger. "I suppose you'd like to witness it for yourself."

Slocum shrugged. "If you'd rather not—"

Hicks laughed loudly. "Just set me up some bottles and stand back," he said.

Slocum did as he was told. He walked to the fencerow and lined up six spare bottles, while Luther Hicks marched to where Slocum had stood previously. Slocum walked over and stood next to the outhouse, watching as Hicks faced the fence. The bottles stood there invitingly, sparkling in the brilliance of the afternoon sun. The sheriff's eyes narrowed into slits as he spat the useless butt of his cigar away. He reached up and scratched his bearded chin, then smoothly dropped his hand to the butt of the Dragoon. The big horse pistol was a blur of walnut and blued steel as Hicks drew it from the holster and fired from the hip.

A thunderous staccato like rapid cannonfire boomed in the warm Kansas air as the .44's hammer struck home six times successively. Slocum shifted his attention to the fencerow in time to see the last bottle shatter beneath the sixth and final slug.

"Does that answer your question?" asked Hicks smugly.

Slocum nodded. "It does," he admitted. Slocum recalled the quickness and ease of Hicks's draw during those days of guerilla fighting on the Kansas-Missouri border, and knew that the man was even more dangerous now than back then. Slocum was fast and accurate, but Hicks still had the advantage, even after all these years. He was still as swift as a rattler's strike.

"All right, now that we've seen what you can do with a six-shooter, let's see how you handle a rifle," said Hicks, absently reloading the Dragoon.

"Just tell me what to do," said Slocum.

Hicks looked around the farm for a moment, then smiled to himself. "See that old windmill over yonder?" he asked, pointing across the dusty barnyard.

Slocum studied the rickety wood windmill that Hicks referred to. It stood on the far side of the barn. Its wheel spun lazily in the breeze, emitting a steady, rusty squeak. "Yeah. What about it?"

"Here's what I want you to do," said Hicks. "Ride to that far ridge, the one we topped on our way here from town."

Slocum looked to the north. The grassy ridge that Hicks spoke of stood a good five hundred yards away. "Then what?"

"When you get there, stay on your horse and aim down on the top of that windmill from the saddle. I count a dozen blades on the hub. If you can knock off eight of the twelve, I'll be satisfied."

Slocum faked an expression of doubt. "That's a pretty far distance. It would take a steady hand and some old-fashioned Kentucky windage."

"Not up to it, eh?" asked Hicks. There was a subtle taunt in the sheriff's stony eyes.

"I didn't say that," said Slocum. He mounted his spotted gelding, then spurred the horse toward the north.

A few minutes later he had reached the top of the ridge. He reined his mount around and faced the farm in the valley below. The spinning rotor of the windmill looked scarcely the size of a coin from that distance.

Slocum reached down and shucked the .44-40 Winchester repeater from its saddle boot. He levered a cartridge into the breech, then lifted the stock to his shoulder. It had been a while since his skill with a rifle had been put to the test so severely. It would be a tricky feat, but he was certain that he could pull it off.

The tall Georgian wet his left thumb and lifted it into the air. The Kansas wind was blowing in from the northwest. The rifle he owned had a folding rear sight fastened to the wrist piece just behind the hammer. Slocum snapped it up, adjusted the sliding gauge for the right trajectory, then leaned into the rifle and lined up both the front and rear sights. He took a bead on the wheel of the windmill and waited for the right moment. It came an instant later. The wind tapered off considerably and the spinning blades slowed a degree.

Slocum released his first shot, shearing a single fin from the circular hub of the windmill. He didn't stop there, fearing that the wind would pick up and spoil his aim. Again and again, he jacked the lever of the repeater and fired. And, again and again, one blade after another dropped from the head of the windmill. Soon, he had shot off eight of the twelve blades that had been required of him. He grinned to himself and continued to fire. Four more shots netted four more blades, bringing the number to an even twelve.

Satisfied, Slocum returned the rifle to its scabbard, then spurred his horse back down the ridge to the farm below. When he got there, he found Luther Hicks standing beneath the supports of the windmill, eyeing the splintered blades that lay in disarray around the structure's base.

"Did I pass?" asked Slocum.

"You sure as hell did," replied Hicks. He pulled his eyes away from the twelve targets and studied Slocum with a mixture of puzzlement and suspicion. "You know, it's been quite a while since I've come across someone who could handle a longarm so well. In fact, I've only known one other man in my lifetime who could do what you can do with a rifle. A rebel sniper back during the war."

Slocum said nothing at first. For a second, he wondered if the strange expression in Hicks's eyes might possibly be one of dawning recognition. "What ever happened to this sniper?" he asked, aware that his question was a gamble and might possibly spark a potentially fatal confrontation.

Just as swiftly, the odd emotion slipped away and Hicks's eyes returned to their former expression of flat disinterest. "He turned traitor and was executed for shaming the name of the Confederacy. But he was a damned good shot, I'll say that. Pert near as good as you are."

As Hicks walked to his horse, eager to head back to town, Slocum watched the big man cautiously. Secretly he breathed a sigh of relief. For a moment he was afraid that the sheriff had recognized him and that his plan to infiltrate the ranks of Judge Burke's nightriders had come to a deadly halt. But it seemed for the time being that Hicks was in the dark as to Slocum's identity.

And, starting back over the ridge toward Tyler's Crossing, Slocum vowed that he would keep Luther Hicks in such an unsuspecting state . . . at least until the right time came to reveal the truth of the matter.

11

It was midafternoon when Slocum and Hicks returned to town. As they reined their horses to a halt in front of the livery stable and began to dismount, Slocum scanned the length of the dusty street. Directly across the street was Pickard's Mercantile and, parked in front of the store, was a rickety flatbed wagon pulled by a lone mule. The wagon might have slipped Slocum's eye if not for one thing. Prissy Kelly was perched on the seat of the buckboard, reins in hand.

As Hicks led his horse into the livery, Slocum lingered outside for a moment longer. He watched as Prissy climbed down off the buckboard and tied the mule to a hitching post. He was surprised that she had made the journey to town alone, given the danger she and her father had dealt with lately. Then she took her father's Henry rifle from the seat beside her and he knew that she wasn't one to take unnecessary chances. The girl had grit, he had to admit that.

Slocum waited until she entered the store, then took his horse to its stable. He shucked the saddle off its back, rubbed it down with hay, then accompanied the sheriff outside.

"Let's head on over to the Plowman," suggested Luther. "That long ride made me thirsty."

Slocum nodded his agreement. As Hicks paused to take one of his cigars from a vest pocket and light it, Slocum looked to the opposite side of the street, hoping to catch another glimpse of Prissy. Instead, he saw Deputy Guthrie pushing the Judge's wheelchair along the boarded sidewalk. Hamilton Burke sat high in his chair, his cold eyes surveying Tyler's Crossing as if it were his own private kingdom. Slocum knew the man probably considered it as such, too.

Burke was almost on the verge of passing the mercantile when he noticed Prissy's buckboard and realized just who it belonged to. A sly, snakelike grin crossed the Judge's bearded face and he directed Guthrie to steer him through the doorway of the general store.

After Hicks had lit his cigar, he and Slocum started up the street for the saloon. When they crossed over to the other sidewalk, Slocum broke away. "Going in the store here for a minute. You go on if you want."

Hicks nodded. "I'll buy us a bottle and have Flanders warm up those cards of his. I aim to win back those greenbacks you took from me yesterday."

Slocum smiled. "We'll see about that." He waited until Hicks was gone, then stood next to the window of the store. He made sure that neither the Judge nor Prissy Kelly saw him enter, then moved through the doorway and ducked into an aisle of dry goods.

Slocum peeked through a crack between two store shelves, getting a fair view of the front of the mercantile. Prissy was standing at the counter, handing a list of articles to the proprietor, Joseph Pickard. As Pickard took the scrap of paper and began to prepare the order, Prissy turned to find the Judge and his gunman standing behind her.

"Pardon me if I startled you, Miss Kelly," said the Judge. "How are you doing today?"

Prissy regarded the man as if he were some particularly ugly type of insect. "Well enough," she said. "Now, if you'll excuse me, I have some more shopping to do."

Burke, however, seemed to have no intention of letting the young woman leave his company so hastefully. "And your father, how is he? I believe he usually comes to town with you, doesn't he?"

"Papa's ailing," said Prissy, although Slocum sensed that the girl was lying. More than likely, Prissy had slipped away from the farm and come to Tyler's Crossing without her father's knowledge. "He's laid up in bed."

The Judge's whiskered features summoned an expression of mock concern. "Aw, I'm sorry to hear that. You do know that your father and I have had an appointment set for the past couple of days, concerning some serious business between he and I, don't you?"

"You mean the business of cheating him out of his money and his land?" asked Prissy boldly. Slocum had to smile at her show of bravado.

The Judge ignored the remark and continued. "When a meeting has been scheduled between myself and someone, I don't normally like to be kept waiting. But if your father is suffering some sickness, I suppose that can't be helped. We will extend our appointment for a few days more . . . and if he's unable to ride to town in that time, I'll be more than happy to send a couple of my deputies out to escort him to the courthouse."

Prissy's face reddened visibly. Her eyes flashing with anger, she stepped up to the Judge, rifle in hand. Startled, Guthrie laid his hand on the butt of his revolver, as if ready to draw against the young brunette. Slocum went one step further and shucked his Colt Navy from its holster. If necessary, he was prepared to shoot Guthrie where he stood, through the space between the store shelves.

"What makes you think you're going to keep on getting what you want and doing as you please here in Tyler's Crossing?" snapped Prissy. Her knuckles were white around the frame of the repeating rifle. "What makes you think someone won't wire the federal marshal and tell him about what you've been up to lately? Or maybe just shoot you dead and get the job over and done with?"

Tension hung heavily between the cluttered walls of the general store. Three hands—two male and one female—clutched gunmetal, ready to put it to deadly use. Then, before emotions could ignite, the Judge's laughter put an end to the potentially explosive situation.

"Really, my dear," chuckled Burke smugly. "If anyone intended to do either one, they would have surely done it by now, don't you think?" When Prissy failed to answer him, he continued. "The truth of the matter is, no one has because they know that they would never be able to get away with it. Notifying a U.S. marshal would be futile. You have no proof for your accusations. As for killing me, there is one sentence and one only for the willful murder of a federal judge, and that is hanging. And I would daresay, neither your father nor any of the other farmers in the area would risk death for the loss of a few measly dollars."

"Whatever you and your filthy nightriders intend to take away from us, Judge Burke, you'll have to fight for it!" declared Prissy. "And when it's all over with, you'll end up empty-handed! I swear to God you will."

Hamilton Burke laughed at Prissy's threat. "I think not, Miss Kelly. You see, I've been doing this for a very long time, in towns exactly like Tyler's Crossing, and I've always gotten everything I've set out to acquire." Burke's gray eyes turned from greed to sudden lust. "And I do mean *everything*, Prissy."

The girl realized the Judge's intentions and recoiled at the mere thought of it. "You disgust me, Burke!" she said. Then, saying nothing more, she walked past him and his henchman and left Pickard's Mercantile. Rifle in hand, Prissy marched down the sidewalk to continue her shopping before the long ride back to the Kelly farm.

For a moment Slocum simply stood and watched. The Judge laughed loudly to himself, Guthrie joining in the mirth. At that instant, Slocum would have liked nothing more than to step around the corner of the shelving and gun them both down. He could have done so with little trouble whatsoever. But, miraculously, he stayed his hand. He returned his Colt to its holster and abstained from the intense desire to kill Burke and Guthrie right there in the general store.

"She'll learn how very serious I am about this matter," the Judge told Guthrie. "They will all learn, sooner or later." Then the two turned and left, exiting the store and continuing their rounds along the single street of Tyler's Crossing.

Slocum waited until both of them were gone, then left his hiding place in the dry goods aisle. He walked to the counter, bought a bag of tobacco and papers from Pickard, and left the store himself. Slocum stood on the sidewalk for a long moment, rolling himself a smoke and watching the Judge make his way gradually back to his castle of a courthouse.

"You may be serious, you old bastard," Slocum said beneath his breath. "But, then, so am I." He lit his cigarette and inhaled deeply, his eyes narrowing. "Dead serious."

And with that, he continued on down the street to the Plowman Saloon.

That afternoon, and on into the night, Slocum sat at the gambling table with Flanders, Sheriff Hicks, and a few others, trying his hand at various games of chance. Lady Luck wasn't smiling on him that day, however. Regardless of his skill with cards or dice, Slocum was unable to gain any ground over Hicks, who seemed to be on a winning streak. The tall Georgian ended up losing twice as much to his opponent as he had won the day before.

Slocum ended up blaming his bad luck on an underlying nervousness. He knew that he would be called to perform the duties of his new job that night, and frankly, he wasn't exactly looking forward to it.

Around a half past ten that night, the batwings of the Plowman Saloon swung open and Guthrie appeared, just as he had the night before. He walked over to the gambling table and, leaning over, whispered something in Hicks's ear.

Although Slocum was sitting on the opposite side of the table, he could still hear what had been said. "The Judge says it's time," was the message Guthrie delivered.

Sheriff Hicks nodded, motioned for his deputies to fold their hands, and stood up. His cold eyes met Slocum's. "Time to earn your pay, Smith," he said.

Slocum said nothing. He simply tossed down his cards— a winning hand to beat all!—and joined the others on their exodus across the barroom.

Silently they left the saloon. Four of the Judge's deputies had been in the Plowman with Hicks and Slocum. Now the others joined them outside, bringing the number to an even dozen. Slocum had seen some of them around town or loitering at the front steps of the courthouse, while others were totally unknown to him. From the suspicious stares he was generating, Slocum knew that he was just as much of a stranger to them.

Moments later they entered the livery stable. Just as with most trustworthy liverymen, Hinchburger had retired early. Slocum could hear his loud snoring echo from the little room he called his home. The sound of Hinchburger's slumber also signified something else to Slocum: that he was solely on his own that night. Whatever happened in the next few hours, it was Slocum's problem and Slocum's alone.

Hicks took a coal-oil lantern from a rusted nail on the wall, lifted the dusty chimney, and lit the wick with a match. Then he motioned for the others to join him at the back of the stable.

Once they had congregated in one of the barn's unoccupied stalls, Hicks spoke in a low voice. "In case any of you are wondering, this here is Smith. He'll be taking Baxter's place."

The gathering of men said nothing in reply. They simply accepted his presence with the air of those who really didn't give a damn. The only one who seemed to take exception to the idea was Guthrie. He gave Slocum an evil look and spat a spritz of tobacco juice into the dust and manure of the stable floor. The brown spittle came a few inches short of splattering the toes of Slocum's boots.

Hicks turned to a long, wooden tool chest in the corner. Crouching next to it, he took a key from his vest pocket and used it to disengage a heavy padlock. Slocum watched as the sheriff took bundles of dark clothing from the chest and passed them out. "Here," said Hicks, handing Slocum a jet-black outfit, complete with dark hat and kerchief. "Baxter was a sight bigger than you, but these duds oughtta fit well enough."

Slocum didn't argue. Like the others, he donned the clothing quietly, until he was dressed in pitch-black from head to toe. The men around him stood silent and solemn, as if they were common brethren in some dark fraternity. Slocum didn't exactly feel the same sense of brotherly belonging, though. He thought of a similar band of night marauders—the white-robed Ku Klux Klan—and knew in his heart that the Judge's nightriders weren't far removed from those who reigned terror in the Southern states east of the Mississippi.

After the men had tightened their gunbelts and checked the loads in their respective pistols, shotguns, and rifles, they filed out the back door. In a corral at the rear of the livery stood a dozen coal-black stallions. Without receiving any type of instruction, the nightriders went to a lean-to and retrieved saddles and gear. Guthrie—who could be distinguished from the others by the bandage on his right hand—took an additional piece of leatherwork with him. Slocum recognized the bullwhip as being the one he had seen the night before at the Jackson farm.

"That one's yours, Smith," indicated Hicks, pointing to a lone stallion at the far end of the corral.

Slocum took a spare saddle from the lean-to and approached the horse. The animal shied away from the stranger at first, but calmed at Slocum's soft words. Soon, he had the riding gear buckled into place and was swinging up into the saddle. He reined the horse to where the others waited by the open gate.

"All right, Smith, listen up," Hicks told him flatly. "You're simply along for the ride tonight. Follow us and try not to get in the way. In any case, just do as you're told and don't ask any questions. Understand?"

"Yes," agreed Slocum, although he couldn't help but wonder just what sort of cruelty they had on their minds that night.

Given the Judge's encounter with Prissy that afternoon, Slocum half expected them to head east toward the Kelly farm. But much to Slocum's relief, they started in the opposite direction.

It was only a few minutes later when Slocum realized exactly where they were going. He rode the same trail he had the night before and, after an hour's journey, ended up back at the farm of Elias Jackson.

Slocum recalled the terror they had subjected the Negro and his family to last night and wondered if he could simply sit there and watch them endure even worse this time. He was afraid that if it came down to it, he would be forced to do just that. To act toward the eleven nightriders would be instant death for him. All were seasoned gunmen who would not be hesitant to put their weapons to fatal use if threatened.

They rode through the surrounding fields of barley and corn, then surrounded the simple sod house. The few windows of the structure were dark; nary a light shone from the other sides of the glass panes.

"Jackson!" called Luther Hicks from the back of his black horse. "Jackson, it's us again! Come on out and let's talk!"

No answer came from within the small house. For all outward appearances, the structure seemed completely unoccupied.

"You were supposed to sign those papers at the courthouse today and you didn't," continued Hicks. "The Judge was mighty peeved about that. Said maybe you needed a little more persuading. Like stringing up one of your young'uns from that tree over yonder. How's that sound to you, Jackson?"

The thought of such a lynching taking place made Slocum's blood run cold. He was certain that he would be unable to restrain himself if Hicks and the others slipped a noose around the neck of one of the Jackson children. Slocum had never been party to the murder of a child and he never would be.

"I don't think the nigger's listening to you," said Guthrie. "Want me to go in there and drag him out?"

Hicks nodded. "Take a couple of men with you. But be careful. He could have himself a gun in there."

Guthrie climbed down off his horse, as did two dark forms Slocum identified as Tipton and McGraw. Together, the three approached the sod house, guns drawn and cocked. Guthrie tried the front door and found it locked. He walked back to his horse, took his shotgun from its saddle boot, then returned to the house. He warned the others to stand clear, then emptied both barrels into the door. The wooden barrier collapsed beneath a hail of double-aught buckshot. An instant later, the three were through the dark doorway and out of view.

Slocum waited, a ball of cold dread forming in the pit of his belly. He snaked his hand off the saddle horn and rested it on the butt of his Navy Colt. If Guthrie and the others emerged with Jackson and one of his children in tow, Slocum knew that he must be prepared to act and act swiftly. Perhaps he could cut down three or four of the nightriders, then escape into the cornfield and keep riding west until he reached Colorado. Even then, he wasn't sure that the Judge would allow him to get off scot-free. Burke seemed like the type who would dog a man relentlessly and make him pay a hundredfold for the wrong that had been done him.

Yes, Slocum was prepared to go to the extreme if necessary, but, fortunately, he was not placed in such an uncompromising position. A moment later Guthrie and the other two left the sod house, shaking their heads in disgust.

"Ain't nobody in there, Hicks," said Guthrie, with an edge of bitter rage in his voice. "Looks like Jackson and his family flew the coop!"

"Damn!" cussed Hicks venomously. "The Judge sure ain't gonna like this none, that's for sure!"

"So, what do you want to do?" asked Guthrie.

Luther Hicks thought for a moment, then replied, "Torch the place. The house, the barn . . . everything. Burn 'em all right down to the ground."

"What about the crops?" asked one of the others.

"We'll hold off on that till I can talk to the Judge," said Hicks.

Several other nightriders dismounted and set to work. Bed sheets were taken from the farmhouse, wound around branches from the oak tree, then doused with coal oil and set afire. With whoops and hollers, they went from one building to another, lighting the dry tinder of prairie grass and weathered lumber.

Helplessly, Slocum sat on his horse and watched as the Jackson farm went up in flames. Soon, the structures were totally engulfed in fire. Thick black smoke and red cinders drifted skyward, and the heat became so intense that the riders were forced to retreat a safe distance from the blazing farm.

Slocum cantered his horse to a halt near the edge of the cornfield and watched as Elias Jackson's dream turned to smoke and ash. A moment later Hicks rode up next to him. "Now you know what the Judge is paying you for," he told Slocum bluntly. "Got any objections?"

"No," Slocum lied. "None at all."

"Good," replied Hicks. " 'Cause next time, you'll be helping out along with the others. Just want to make sure you ain't gonna go yellow on us."

"I'll do what needs to be done," said Slocum.

"Make sure you do," warned Hicks. Then, motioning for the other nightriders to follow, he sent his stallion toward the east in a steady gallop.

Slocum let the others ride ahead of him, then followed. As they left the field of high summer corn and topped a ridge, Slocum turned in his saddle and looked back down at the Jackson farm. The fire still burned brightly and probably would until morning.

As he made the long journey back to Tyler's Crossing, Slocum felt badly about taking part in the destruction of the farm. But he vowed that he would make up for it in some way . . . to Elias Jackson and all the other farmers that the Judge and his nightriders were victimizing so cruelly and without conscience.

12

It was well past midnight when the nightriders finally returned to Tyler's Crossing.

They rode silently, avoiding the main street and making their way as quietly as a dozen black shadows along the southern outskirts of town. When they reached the corral at the rear of the livery stable, they dismounted, led their horses through by the reins, then quickly unsaddled them. Then the band of nocturnal guerillas entered the barn and removed their black outfits, dressing in their own clothing. When Luther Hicks had snapped the padlock in place on the wooden chest, they walked stealthfully through the building to the front entrance. The liveryman seemed oblivious to their presence, however. Hinchburger's snoring sounded even deeper than it had several hours before.

No one said a word of farewell. The twelve disbanded, each man drifting away into the night to their respective beds. Slocum walked a ways toward the Plowman Saloon, then paused in the shadow of a storefront when he was sure that he wasn't being watched by any of the others. He stood there for a few minutes, then carefully backtracked to the livery.

The moment he entered the structure, he noticed that the sound of the liveryman's snoring no longer echoed from the side room. He walked up to the inner door and spoke. "Hinchburger?"

"I'm awake," came the voice of the blacksmith. He opened the door and beckoned for Slocum to come in. "I have been since you fellows rode out. I was just playing possum."

"I don't blame you," said Slocum. "This is a cold-blooded bunch we're dealing with. Wouldn't do for them to know you were privy to their comings and goings."

"So," asked Hinchburger, stoking some more wood into the fire of his potbelly stove, "how did it go tonight?"

"We paid a visit to Elias Jackson," said Slocum.

Hinchburger's bushy eyebrows raised a degree. "That Negro farmer out west of town?"

"Yes," said Slocum. "Luckily for him and his family, they'd already deserted the farm by the time we got there."

"And I assume that peeved Hicks to no end."

Slocum nodded. "They burnt every building on the place to the ground. Left only the crops standing."

"The lousy sons of bitches," grumbled Hinchburger in disgust. He eyed Slocum curiously. "And what did you do? Did you help them?"

"No, I just sat there on my horse and watched. And didn't do a damned thing to stop them."

Hinchburger shook his head. "Nothing you could've done, friend. If you'd made one wrong move against them, they'd have doused you with coal oil and set you on fire along with everything else."

"You're right about that," agreed the tall Georgian. "I was only a spectator tonight, but next time they might want me to join in. And I'm not sure I can bring myself to do that."

"I can tell that it's a burr under your saddle, riding with these bastards," said the liveryman. "Maybe you'd best saddle up that gelding of yours and get out of town while you still can. I wouldn't think any less of you if you decided to."

"No," said Slocum, "but I would. I have to find some way to stop the Judge and his thugs from getting what they want."

Hinchburger scratched his rusty red beard. "I doubt there's any way that one man could do that without getting killed in the process. Truthfully, the only way to knock a powerful man like the Judge down off his throne is to fight fire with fire."

"You mean use the law against him," guessed Slocum.

"Right," said the blacksmith. "If you could get hold of the federal marshal in Fort Atkinson, he'd probably have the Judge disbarred and thrown in prison before much more damage could be done."

"But like you said before, Burke has the post office and telegraph in his control. How else could we get word to the marshal without going to Fort Atkinson ourselves?"

"There's a coach station about a half day's ride southwest of here," said Hinchburger. "Little watering hole called Shaffer's Gulch. If you could ride there and leave a message with the caretaker, he could probably pass it on to the coach driver and have him send it by telegraph when he reached Russell City a few days later."

"Why haven't you tried it before?" asked Slocum.

Hinchburger laughed. " 'Cause I'd be a dead man if I did. The Judge depends on me to take care of those horses of his. I'm the only liveryman in town, and if I was to up and disappear even for a few hours, he and his bogus lawmen would get suspicious. They'd find out where I went and punish me for my disloyalty . . . with a bullet in my brain pan, no doubt."

Slocum knew that he was right. Someone as depended on as Hinchburger couldn't possibly slip out of town and summon help. And as for Slocum making the ride, he wouldn't be able to do it either, at least not until Hicks and the other nightriders grew less suspicious of him. When they grew to trust him and take him for granted, then maybe Slocum could get away with some form of deceptive action.

"So what do you plan to do, Smith?" asked Hinchburger. "Are you going to keep riding with them . . . or hightail out of here?"

"I reckon I'll stick around for the duration," said Slocum. "Even if I end up regretting it."

"Remember, I'm here whenever you need my help," offered the liveryman.

"Just be ready to saddle my horse at a moment's notice, that's all I ask."

"You've got it." The two shook hands to seal their common alliance against the Judge.

Quietly Slocum left the livery stable. He slipped from shadow to shadow, until he finally reached the outer stairway of the Plowman Saloon. He entered the side entrance to find the place dark and unoccupied. Unnoticed, Slocum made his way along the upper landing to his door.

As he slipped inside, he half expected to encounter Charlene, naked and waiting for him beneath the sheets, the same as the night before. But the blond whore was obviously sharing her bed with someone else that evening. Slocum's bed was empty.

In a way, Slocum was thankful for the solitude. He had a lot on his mind after his first nightride with Hicks and the others, and he needed some peace in which to think things out. He quietly undressed and lay down. Slocum attempted to devise some plan to thwart Burke's plans, but it seemed that the long ride had exhausted him more than he thought. A few minutes later he was fast asleep.

The following day Slocum spent his time hobnobbing with those he had ridden with the night before.

For breakfast he bought a bottle of whiskey and shared the bartender's breakfast of biscuits and red-eye gravy with Luther Hicks and several other of Burke's hired guns. Then he walked over to the courthouse and visited with those who loafed on the front steps. They were cool toward him at first, but after a while they grudgingly accepted him into their ranks. Most appeared to have fought on the side of the Confederacy during the war and that forged a common bond between them. They swapped stories of battles and skirmishes, their victories as well as defeats. Slocum had to change the places and circumstances of his own wartime experiences, though. If he had given them the true details, some might have recognized him. During those years of conflict between North and South, the exploits of John Slocum had not been unknown among those who had served under Generals Lee, Jackson, and Bragg.

As the morning drew on into afternoon, Slocum spent his time back at the Plowman, gambling for low stakes with Flanders and anyone else with an itch for poker. Around five o'clock, Slocum grew weary of playing cards and went upstairs to his room. He lay down and, with the help of a quarter bottle of whiskey, took a long and sound nap.

He awoke to the rapping of knuckles on his door. Slocum was startled at first. It was pitch-dark in the room. He reached over to the bedpost, found where his gunbelt hung there, and shucked the Colt Navy from its holster. "Who is it?" he demanded.

"Guthrie," came the voice of the pale-eyed deputy. "Hicks sent me up to tell you that it's time."

"I'm coming," said Slocum. Quickly he pulled on his boots, fastened his gunbelt around his waist, and grabbed his hat off the bedpost. He shook the last sluggishness of sleep from his mind, the thought of riding with Hicks and the others pumping a shot of adrenaline through his veins. He wondered what sort of mischief they had planned for tonight.

He stepped out onto the upstairs landing, squinting against the brilliance of kerosene lanterns. He glanced over to the wall clock and saw that the time was a few minutes past the hour of ten.

Hicks and the others were waiting for him on the porch of the saloon. "Next time be ready to go," was all that Hicks said before they started down the street toward the livery stable.

Their ritual was identical to the one they had followed the night before. They sneaked past the sleeping liveryman, donned their black clothing, then saddled their horses. When everyone was ready, they opened the corral gate and left, one by one.

This time they traveled neither east nor west. They headed due north, where the Kansas plains seemed to stretch, totally flat and even, for miles. After nearly an hour of riding, they came upon lush fields of alfalfa and wheat, stretching as far as the eye could see. A half-moon was out that night, casting a pale glow upon the unbroken horizon. As they rode along a narrow trail, Slocum spied the peaked roofs of several buildings in the distance. He breathed deeply, preparing himself for whatever violence Hicks and Guthrie had cooked up for that night's invasion.

Soon, they were galloping through a dusty barnyard and reining to a stop outside a two-story farmhouse. Luther Hicks raised his voice, calling out to someone inside. "Will Sutherland! Come out here and face us!"

"Go to hell!" cursed a gruff voice from the upper story of the farmhouse. There was the crash of broken glass, then the sharp crack of a rifle. Dust erupted beneath the hooves of Hicks's stallion, making the dark horse prance and paw like a dancehall girl.

Hicks motioned to three of the riders to go around back. As they obeyed his orders, he drew his Dragoon from its holster and snapped a couple of shots at the window. The .44 slugs tore away fragments of the window frame, but nothing more. "You'd best put down that rifle and come on out, Sutherland.

If you don't, we'll be forced to come in and get you."

"Just you try!" yelled the farmer. Another rifle shot rang out. The bullet tugged at Hicks's high-peaked hat, knocking it off his head.

"Damn that crazy sodbuster!" said Hicks. "Looks like he's gonna be as stubborn about signing those papers as Jackson was!" He motioned for the others to join him at the barn at the opposite end of the dirt yard. As they made the shelter of the barn, the roar of gunfire sounded at the rear of the house. The three who had tried to gain entrance at the back door were fleeing like a pack of scalded dogs.

"What's going on?" demanded Hicks angrily.

"It's Sutherland's wife," said one of the nightriders. "She was waiting for us with a shotgun. Peppered Caldwell right good before we could get clear."

One of the three riders held a gloved hand to his backside. "Ain't nothing," he grimaced, trying to conceal the pain of his wounds. "Just a little birdshot, that's all."

Luther Hicks mulled his options over in his mind, then turned to Slocum. "Got a job for you, Smith," he said. "I want you to climb to the peak of this here barn and try to get a shot at Sutherland the next time he shows himself at that window. You ought to be able to manage that, don't you think?"

Slocum didn't cotton to the idea of having to shoot an innocent man, but he was careful not to let his feelings show. "I'll give it a try," he said.

"You do that," said Hicks. "Just pretend he's sitting on top of a windmill."

Slocum climbed down off his black stallion, shucked his Winchester from its boot, and left the others. He walked around the far end of the barn and found an access way to the steep-pitched roof of the tall structure—a toolshed that was built onto the rear wall. Carefully he made his way to the top of the shed, then onto the eaves of the barn. A few moments later Slocum was creeping on his belly along the junction beam of the roof, until he was overlooking the front of the Sutherland house.

He cocked his rifle and laid his cheek against the stock, sighting down the length of the barrel. A second later one of the nightriders broke away from the concealment of the barn. The lone horseman spurred his mount in front of the farmhouse, whooping and hollering, firing a brace of twin Remington revolvers at the upper story.

Regretfully Slocum centered the sights of the Winchester on the upstairs window that the farmer had fired from upon the nightriders' arrival. He waited for only an instant. Then Will Sutherland appeared at the window with a big Sharps buffalo rifle in his hands. It was dark, but the sparse moonlight shone on the white of the farmer's nightshirt, giving Slocum a definite target.

Slocum could have killed the man. He could have put a .44 slug directly in the man's heart or clean through the center of his forehead. But he wasn't about to commit cold-blooded murder in order to save his own skin. Instead, he shifted his aim slightly and unleashed a single shot. The bullet hit Will Sutherland in the bicep of his left arm. The shock of the wound spun the farmer on his feet, knocking the big Sharps completely out of his grasp. Instead of falling backward, Sutherland pitched forward. He fell through the open window, rolled off the eaves of the front porch, and landed with a thud on the ground below.

The Georgian was relieved to see the man roll over a moment after he had hit the earth. Slocum didn't feel very proud of what he had just done, but at least the injury he had inflicted wasn't a fatal one. And the fall from the upstairs window seemed to have only knocked the wind from the farmer.

By the time Slocum made his way down off the barn, Hicks and the others had congregated in front of the farm-house. Her husband's injury had taken all the fight out of Marjory Sutherland. She had discarded her shotgun and rushed to Will's side. But she didn't remain there long. One of the nightriders roughly pulled her away and, tossing her back into the house, blocked the door.

Hicks stood over Sutherland, staring down at the gun-shot farmer and shaking his masked head. "That was a mighty foolish thing to do," he told the man. Cruelly he bore the heel of his boot down on Sutherland's bullet wound, causing the man to thrash. Will Sutherland was a proud man, however. He refused to scream. He merely groaned between tightly clenched teeth.

The leader of the nightriders removed his boot from Sutherland's arm and knelt beside the injured man. "You're starting to rub me the wrong way, Sutherland," Hicks told him. "We were out here about a week ago and we told you plain and simple what you had to do. You were to visit the Judge the next day and sign those papers he had waiting for you at his office. But did you show up? Hell no! You did like all those other addle-brained sodbusters. You ignored us, thought we were just joking around with you. Well, you learned different tonight, didn't you? You learned that what we told you was the gospel truth."

"You mean the gospel according to Burke?" spat Suther-land bitterly. "I take no one's gospel to heart, other than that of the Lord Almighty!"

"You Bible-thumpers are all the same," growled Hicks. "You always want to take the hard road and suffer like ole Job did. Well, if you want to suffer, Sutherland, we'll sure be happy to oblige you." Hicks nodded to a couple of the nightriders. "Lash him to that porch post there."

Sutherland struggled, but the blood he had lost had sapped him of his strength. A moment later he was tied securely to the post, his back to the gathering of dark riders.

Hicks nodded in approval, then turned to Guthrie. "Give him a taste of the whip," he said. "Maybe that'll burn some sense into that stubborn head of his."

Guthrie stepped forward. He reached out and tore the flannel nightshirt off Sutherland's back, exposing the man's naked flesh. Then Guthrie shifted the coil of braided leather to his good hand, unfurled the ten-foot whip, and reared back powerfully, preparing to administer the first blow.

Slocum felt a lump rise to his throat. More than anything else he wanted to stop this from happening. He wanted to draw his pistol and gun down the sadistic man named Guthrie. But he didn't. He had no choice but to simply stand there and watch as the tall fellow with the pale eyes and the bullwhip went to work.

The bullwhip fell a dozen times before the beating finally stopped. When the torture had ended, Will Sutherland's back was a mass of bloody stripes. The farmer had maintained his willpower up until the eighth lash. Then he could contain his agony no longer and his silent rebellion had given way to shrill screaming. Slocum had averted his eyes during the horsewhipping, but he could do nothing to drive the sound of Sutherland's screams away.

Afterward, Hicks walked back up to the sobbing farmer and grabbed him by the hair of the head. "We ain't unreasonable men, Sutherland. We're willing to give you another chance. You've got two more days to get to town and sign those papers. After that, we'll come back. And if we have to, we'll take the whip to your old lady? Do you understand?"

Sutherland nodded quietly.

"Good. I'm glad to hear that," replied Hicks. He turned toward his band of nightriders. "Come on, boys. Let's get out of here."

Silently they mounted their black horses and prepared to leave. As Slocum swung into his saddle, Hicks rode up. Above his black kerchief, Slocum could see the gleam of satisfaction in Hicks's flat gray eyes. "Good shooting," he said, then galloped away, leading the others southward back to town.

Slocum said nothing in reply. He simply sat in the saddle for a long moment and stewed angrily in the face of Hicks's commendation. He felt no pride whatsoever in what he had done that night, only shame and self-disgust. Slocum had regretted using his gun a number of times in the past, but this time beat all the others. He had shot a man in order to protect his own hide.

As he spurred his horse to follow the others, John Slocum vowed to himself that he would never put himself into such a situation again. He knew it would be more honorable to take a bullet himself than to be forced to shoot an innocent man again.

13

The same as the night before, Slocum lingered behind after he and the other nightriders had returned to town, put their horses and black clothing away, and disbanded. He clung to the shadows next to the livery stable, waiting for the other gunmen to vanish into the darkness. Then he stepped back inside and walked directly to Hinchburger's room. The burly liveryman was sitting next to the stove, waiting for him.

"I've had enough," said Slocum, accepting a cup of tar-black coffee from the big blacksmith.

"It was worse tonight, wasn't it?" observed Hinchburger. He studied the anguished expression on Slocum's face and knew instantly that the tall Georgian had been railroaded into doing something that he now regretted.

"Yes, it was," replied Slocum. Briefly he detailed that night's events, including his having to shoot Will Sutherland from the roof of the barn.

"I was afraid it'd come to that," said Hinchburger. "You were bound to have to prove yourself sooner or later. So, what do you aim to do now?"

Slocum emptied his cup with a long swallow, then cast the dregs into the open slits of the stove door. The wood fire hissed as the wet grounds hit the flames. "Saddle my horse for me," he said. "Then tell me how to get to that coach station you were telling me about."

Hinchburger nodded his shaggy head in approval. "But what about Hicks and the others? Could be right dangerous for you if they were to find out where you went and what you were up to."

"I'll deal with that later," said Slocum. "Right now, I just want to put a stop to this damned business and then head on to Colorado like I first intended."

"Then I'll saddle that horse for you," said Hinchburger, rising from his chair. "If you ride out now, you'll get to that station by dawn and more than likely be back here a little after noon."

While the liveryman readied Slocum's gelding, the tall Georgian gathered up staples for his trip; a canteen of water from the trough outside and some jerky and leftover cornbread from the pantry in Hinchburger's living quarters. By the time he reached the corral at the rear of the stable, the spotted horse was already saddled and ready to go.

"Take care, Smith," said Hinchburger, shaking the man's hand. Then he watched as the drifter with the Colt Navy headed southwest into the night. Soon, the darkness had swallowed him whole and he was gone.

The early light of morning found Slocum riding the flat, scrubby plains of western Kansas. Despite his ride to the Sutherland farm the night before, he felt awake and alert. The nap he had taken in his room at the Plowman Saloon had helped quite a bit.

On toward six o'clock, he saw a stand of green cedars and a single building ahead. A weathered sign by the side of the trail proclaimed SHAFFER'S GULCH STATION—ONE HALF MILE. Eager to accomplish his secretive task and get back to Tyler's Crossing before he was missed, Slocum spurred his horse forward. The animal quickened its pace, and before long, they were there.

The place wasn't much to look at, but then most stations that catered to the needs of the stagecoaches and their passengers were more functional than comfortable. The single structure was constructed of dust-scrubbed boards and sported a long porch along its front. The porch looked to be where weary travelers congregated and ate their meals. There were several cane-backed rocking chairs there, as well as a long oak table with hand-carved benches. On the far side of the station, beneath the shade of a spreading chestnut tree, stood a large three-seat outhouse that provided relief of a different sort.

Next to the coach station was a broad corral holding a couple dozen horses. The geldings and mares were sturdy and well taken care of, the kind of animals the coach lines of the Overland and Butterfield preferred for their teams. There were also a few mules—Missouri-bred, from the looks of them—obviously kept for any freight wagons that might pass through Shaffer's Gulch and be in need of fresh animals.

Slocum reined his horse to a halt at a hitching rail out front of the station. As he swung down from the saddle, a grizzled man of perhaps eighty stepped spryly onto the porch, tugging the suspenders of his filthy britches over his skinny shoulders. He was as bald as a billiard ball, but his lower face seemed to make up for his hairless scalp. He had a long white beard that reached clear to the belly of his faded red long johns.

The elderly man sucked on the stem of a corncob pipe and eyed Slocum suspiciously. "Can I help you with something, mister?"

"Are you the caretaker here?" asked Slocum flatly.

The old man nodded. "That I am. Charlie Canton's the name." He waited for the dark-haired stranger to return the introduction but he didn't. "I was just fixing to rustle up some breakfast. Not much more than flapjacks and hog jowl bacon, but you're more than welcome to join me, if you want."

"Much obliged," said Slocum. He had eaten a little of the jerky and cold cornbread, but it didn't satisfy him the way a hot meal would. He stepped up on the porch, respectfully removed his hat, then sat down on one of the benches. He took the makings from his shirt pocket and rolled himself a cigarette while the old man returned inside to cook breakfast.

A short time later Charlie Canton returned to the porch holding an iron skillet of hotcakes and bacon in one hand and a steaming coffeepot and two tin cups in the other. Canton joined Slocum at the table, and for a few moments they feasted on the food and hot coffee without engaging in conversation. Then the caretaker's curiosity got the better of him. "You aiming to wait around for the coach, stranger?" he finally asked.

"No, I'll be heading back to Tyler's Crossing in a while," said Slocum. "But the stage is partly why I'm here. I have a message I need to send by telegraph and I was figuring maybe the driver of the next coach might do the job for me at the next town, if I left a gold piece or two for his trouble."

"I'm pretty sure he would," said Canton. He eyed Slocum beneath bushy brows. "But Tyler's Crossing has a telegraph office. Why don't you send it through there?"

Slocum didn't know quite how to explain without revealing too much. "Well, there's been some trouble back in town and the message I'm sending might stir it up a bit, if it got back to the wrong pair of ears."

Canton crammed a long strip of hog jowl into his whiskered mouth and chewed it with the few teeth he had left. "By trouble, I reckon you're talking about Judge Harrison Burke."

The caretaker's revelation put Slocum on guard. "How would you know about the Judge's doings?"

"You tend to hear a lot working a job like this one," said Canton. "Besides, I have kin who live near Tyler's Crossing. My nephew's a wheat farmer by the name of Archie Canton. Would you know him?"

"Afraid not," said Slocum.

"This message you're wanting to send, does it concern the Judge and what he's been trying to do?"

Slocum felt like he could trust the old man, so he took a scrap of paper from his pocket and passed it across the table. "Read it for yourself," he invited.

Canton squinted at the note for a second, then fished a pair of wire-rimmed spectacles from his britches pocket. "Hmmm," he said in interest. "So it's going clear to the state marshal in Fort Atkinson, eh?"

"That's right," replied Slocum, wondering if he might have made a mistake taking the elderly caretaker into his confidence.

"Well, now, I'll tell you what, stranger," said Canton. "The next stage is due in late this afternoon. I'll make sure the driver takes this message on to the next town and sends it off by telegraph just as soon as he gets there." When Slocum started to lay a few coins down to pay for the service, Canton waved the money away. "Don't worry about that. If the driver needs to be paid, I'll do it . . . as a favor to my nephew."

"I understand," said Slocum. He took two bits from his pocket and laid it on the table in front of the old man. "But let me pay for the vittles, if nothing else."

Charlie Canton shrugged his bony shoulders and took the money. "If you insist."

As Slocum rose to go, Canton spoke out. "This trouble in Tyler's Crossing . . . is it as bad as I've heard?"

"Worse, more than likely," said Slocum. "But, hopefully, with your help we can stop it before someone ends up getting killed."

"Don't worry," assured Canton. "I'll see that the message gets sent, even if I have to saddle up my mule and ride to the nearest telegraph office myself."

"Much obliged," said Slocum in parting.

Slocum untethered his gelding, swung into the saddle, and reined his mount back toward the east. As he headed back to Tyler's Crossing, he looked around and saw Charlie Canton leave the porch and walk to the corral to tend to the horses. Slocum thought about the time it would take for the stage-coach driver to deliver the message to the next town and the distance of the telegraph relay itself. It could be several days or even a week before the marshal in Fort Atkinson arrived in Tyler's Crossing to put the power-hungry Judge in his rightful place.

And Slocum knew a lot could happen in that time . . . including outright murder. Whether it turned out to be that of a rebellious farmer or Slocum himself depended on how well the Georgian could keep up the charade he had been playing since joining up with the Judge's nightriders several days ago.

14

Upon his return to Tyler's Crossing, Slocum avoided taking the direct route into town. He rode a couple of miles south of the community, then made a gradual swing toward the eastern limits in a way that would be less conspicuous than simply riding smack down the middle of main street. As far as he could tell, he reached the rear of the livery stable without anyone being the wiser.

Slocum tethered his spotted gelding in the corral out back, then slipped around the side of the building to the blacksmith shop. Just as he expected, Hinchburger was busily at work. As he labored over a wagon wheel that he was repairing, the liveryman heard the sound of Slocum's footsteps but didn't turn around.

"Is it done?" he asked.

"Yes," replied Slocum, sticking to the gloom of the overhang. "I left my horse in the corral out back."

Hinchburger nodded. "I'll take care of it. Now you'd best get on over to the Plowman before anybody else starts missing you."

"What do you mean?" asked the tall Georgian.

"Hicks and a couple of his men were over here around nine," the blacksmith told him. "Said they had a few errands to run for the Judge and were wondering where you were. I told them I didn't rightly know, but they insisted on checking your horse's stall anyway. Seemed kind of peeved when they found it empty."

"Damn," was all that Slocum said on the matter.

"Don't worry," assured Hinchburger. "You might be able to bluff your way out of it before they get suspicious. But if I was you, I'd get over to the saloon and smooth things over as soon as I could."

Slocum backed out of the smithy and made his way along the rear of the buildings that stretched along the town's southern side. When he reached the alleyway that exited opposite the Plowman Saloon, he took that route and was soon crossing the street to the drinking establishment. At first he considered sneaking in the side entrance, but knew that Hicks would confront him with his absence sooner or later. So, instead, he chose to get it over and done with. He pushed through the batwing doors and walked right into the barroom.

Luther Hicks and a few of his deputies were standing at the bar, sipping mugs of warm beer. "Well, look here, boys," said Hicks with more than a little sarcasm in his voice. "Just who we were looking for."

Slocum stepped up to the bar and ordered a bottle and a glass from Henry. "Oh, really?" he countered nonchalantly. He took the whiskey from the bartender, pulled the cork with his teeth, then poured himself a drink.

"Yeah," said Hicks. "The Judge had a few errands he wanted us to run this morning. But when we came looking for you around nine o'clock, you were nowhere to be found. We even went down to the livery just to see if your horse was still there. It wasn't."

Another man might have lost his nerve at the expression of suspicious accusation in the bearded man's stone-gray eyes, but not Slocum. He stared back at the man flatly. "Is there some kind of law around here about a man taking a morning ride? Leaving this stinkhole of a town and getting off to himself for a while?"

Hicks backed off a little, sensing the Georgian's rising anger. "Well, no, that ain't the point. We all tend to do that every now and then, especially men like us who are more at home on the range than cooped up between four walls. But one of the conditions of working for the Judge was that you were to be ready anytime, day or night, to do whatever Burke might want. I've got to warn you, Smith, the Judge wasn't too happy when he found out you were out gallivanting around."

"Without his permission, you mean?" asked Slocum. He played his apparent indignation for all it was worth. "Well, you can tell the Judge that I don't play that game. When we're on a job, like last night, fine, I'll do what I'm being paid to do. But any other time, I'm my own man, and that means riding clear from here to Mexico if I have a mind to."

Slocum could tell that the others' opinion of him had risen a notch from the time he had entered the saloon. Their suspicion had given away to a grudging admiration. In their eyes, Slocum had only given in to the overpowering urge to break away from the mundane setting of Tyler's Crossing and taken an innocent ride on the open prairie, something that they would have all preferred doing more often than they actually did. Only Hicks seemed to hang on to his suspicions a moment longer, wondering if the drifter might have been up to no good. But an instant later, Hicks smiled broadly and shook his head.

"Headstrong bastard, ain't you?" he said.

Slocum was relieved that his act had fooled them, but refused to let his guard down quite so quickly. "I suppose so," he said. "But next time you come looking for me, just remember that you ain't my lord and master just because you hold the reins on those midnight rides of ours."

"Fair enough," said Hicks. He lowered his voice a bit. "Speaking of our work, we'll likely be riding out again tonight."

Slocum nodded and took a long, burning swallow of red-eye. "I'll be ready."

"That's good to know," said the big Missourian. " 'Cause we might just need that straight-shooting rifle of yours, just like last night." Hicks eyed the dark-haired Southerner curiously. "Tell me something, Smith. Why did you choose to wing Sutherland in the arm? You could just as easily shot him between the eyes, dead center."

"I knew you wanted him alive," said Slocum. "Just like that farmer Jackson, you mentioned something about him signing some papers for the Judge. And I figured it would be mighty hard for a dead man to climb out of his casket and sign his name, now wouldn't it?"

Hicks and the others laughed uproariously. "Yeah, I reckon so! That would be quite a feat to manage, even for a God-fearing fella like old Sutherland!"

The men's amusement laid Slocum's anxiety to rest, if only for the time being. Nothing else was said on the matter of his brief absence during the remainder of the afternoon, and needless to say, Slocum was glad that conversation was turned toward other topics of interest and away from him and his mysterious ride that morning.

On toward five o'clock, Slocum broke away from the company of Luther Hicks and the others and made his way toward the staircase that would take him to the upper floor. As he had drank his way leisurely through his bottle of rye whiskey, Slocum had noticed Charlene making her rounds through the barroom, flirting with those who congregated there. She had hooked a couple of johns and lured them to her room upstairs.

The thought of being with the busty blonde again nagged at Slocum and he knew that he wanted her one more time before he left Tyler's Crossing. The odds were against his having a lengthy stay in the little Kansas town and he knew he might have to pull up stakes and leave before he was ready, especially if that night's activity required him to draw his sights on an innocent farmer again. He was certain he would rather lay spurs to his horse and make a run for it before he was forced to do that again.

The last Slocum had seen of Charlene had been close to a half hour ago. She had whispered something to Henry, then gone to her quarters upstairs. Twenty minutes later the bartender had appeared from a room behind the bar toting two large wooden buckets filled to the brim with steaming hot water. As he climbed the stairs with a bucket in each hand, Slocum had a fairly good idea what the water was being used for. So, when Henry had again returned to his duties behind the bar, Slocum figured he would take a break from the monotony of the evening and pay the fair-haired whore a visit.

When he reached Charlene's door, he knocked lightly.

He heard the gentle shift of water on the other side of the wooden barrier. "Sorry, but I'm off-duty," she called out. "I've had my fill of horny men for today. Try again tomorrow."

Slocum smiled to himself. "I'm not sure I can hold out that long," he said so only she could hear.

"John?" she asked sprightly. The weariness in her voice had suddenly vanished. "Please, do come in."

Slocum turned the brass knob and entered Charlene's room. A single lamp was lit, the wick turned down until only a muted glow filled the room. The furnishings looked to have been imported from back East; a huge brass-framed bed with silken sheets, an ornately carved side table and mirrored chifforobe, as well as frilly curtains and a delicately painted dressing screen. Charlene's daytime apparel—her ruffled bloomers, lacy bodice, and shear black stockings hung over the top of the screen, where she had placed them only a few moments before.

He shut the door behind him, then regarded the woman herself. Charlene sat in a long tin bathtub in the center of the room. Her long blond hair was pulled tightly into a bun on the top of her head and most of her body was concealed beneath soapy suds. All that he could see was her long, swanlike neck, her milky shoulders, and the prominent slope of her chest. The brown circles of her nipples peeked slightly through the tiny bubbles. Slocum felt the crotch of his britches tighten at the sight of those teasing buds.

"I was wondering if you'd feel the urge for me again," Charlene said with a mock pout of full red lips. "I was beginning to believe that you hadn't enjoyed our time together the other night."

"Nothing could be further from the truth," said Slocum. "I've just been busy, that's all."

"Yes, I heard that you signed up with the Judge's bunch," said the whore.

"Do you disapprove?" asked Slocum.

The woman shrugged, the movement giving the drifter a better view of her breasts before they again returned below the mound of bubbles. "It doesn't make any difference to me," she said. "I'm more accustomed to dealing with what's between a man's legs than what lies in his heart. I'm certainly not going to lecture you like some fire-and-brimstone preacher."

"Glad to hear that," said Slocum, taking a couple of steps closer. "I sure didn't come in here with religion on my mind, that's for sure."

Charlene smiled seductively at him, then lifted her right leg. Her shapely foot rose, dripping, from the depths of the tub. The big toe beckoned toward him. "Then come on over here, John."

Slocum did as he was told. However, the closer he came to the tub, the more the blonde wrinkled her pretty nose. "I don't mean to offend you, lover, but you stink like a polecat. When was the last time you had a decent bath?"

The drifter's face reddened in embarrassment. "Come to think of it, I don't rightly recall."

"Then I suggest you shed those nasty clothes and join me," she said. "I think there's enough room in here for two."

Slocum didn't need to be asked twice. He shucked his shirt, britches, and boots, tossing them into a pile on the bedroom floor. Soon, he stood there next to the bathtub, completely naked from head to toe. Charlene reached out with a soapy hand and wrapped her wet fingers around his prick. It was already erect and jutting eagerly.

She gave him a firm squeeze. "Well, don't be shy. Join me."

Slocum stepped into the tub. The water was still hot; he could feel the heat of it against his feet and shins. At Charlene's gentle urging, he sat down in the oval basin, facing the beautiful saloon girl. The warm water should have had a relaxing effect on him and normally it would have. But the closeness of the whore and the way she worked her hand up and down the shaft of his manhood beneath the sudsy surface of the water only heightened his excitement. He felt his lust building until his urge for her was nearly maddening.

When he leaned toward her, Charlene placed a restraining palm against his hairy chest. "No," she whispered. "Just lay back and enjoy yourself."

Slocum did as he was told, knowing that whatever she had in mind would be well worth it. He lay back and rested the back of his head against the curved lip of the tub.

Charlene rose from her sitting position until she was perched on her knees. Slocum stared at her large tits, glistening with bubbles and water, and he ached even more, wanting nothing more than to reach out and grab them, draw them to his mouth. But a gentle shake of her head told him to wait until later.

Her hands rose from beneath the water. One held a large bar of white soap, while the other held a washcloth. With a wicked grin, Charlene soaped up the rag and began to run it slowly over Slocum's shoulders and chest. Slocum groaned softly at the touch of the soapy cloth against his skin. It had been a long time since he had felt anything quite as soothing and sensual as the scrubbing the blond whore was currently subjecting him to.

When she had finished with his upper body, Charlene started with his lower. Beneath the surface of the water, she worked with the slick soap bar, running it along his feet, his ankles, the shins of his legs. When the teasing block of soap passed his knees and traveled up his inner thighs, Slocum shifted his weight, straining toward her magical hands. He could feel himself swelling and lengthening beneath the water, every nerve ending pushed toward the brink of exploding.

Right when he anticipated the touch of the soap against his cock, Charlene pulled the bar away teasingly. Instead, she left her kneeling position and stood. Slocum stared at the lush thatch of golden curls at her crotch and saw that it glistened with something more than soap and water. He reached out and ran a finger along her opening. Slocum knew instantly that she was as ready for him as he was for her.

Gripping the sides of the bathtub, Charlene mounted his straining hips, then lowered herself. Slocum slid into her with no trouble at all. The saloon girl moaned. "You're . . . you're so *big!*" were the only words she could manage. She hesitated for a moment, allowing herself to grow accustomed to his size, then she began to work her hips up and down. The slosh of the bathwater and the moist sound of her natural juices filled Slocum's ears. He felt as though he were making love in the middle of the Rio Grande.

As Charlene's pace began to quicken, he found the blonde's breasts in close proximity to his mouth. He fastened his lips around the tip of one and sucked hard. The nipple turned harder than a bullet. Slocum tasted soap, but he didn't care. As he drew moans of pleasure from the wanton woman, he abandoned the breast he had been working on and started on the other.

The urgency of both increased, until neither could bear it any longer. Slocum began to buck upward as Charlene slid downward. The turbulence the two caused sent waves of soapy water sloshing over the walls of the tub and onto the boards of the bedroom floor. They were oblivious to the ruckus they were causing. Slocum felt his sap began to rise and knew by the way Charlene's body tensed that she was on the brink of ecstasy also.

Their cries of passion rose and mingled until they sounded like one single shriek. Then, as the shared sensation reached its pinnacle and leveled off, they slumped back into the tub, exhausted.

Slocum and Charlene lay there in the warm water for a while, saying nothing, simply enjoying the closeness of each other. Then the clock on the outer landing struck the hour of eight and he knew he must prepare himself for that night's ride. Reluctantly he pulled himself away from Charlene and stepped from the tub. He quickly toweled off and dressed.

"Thanks for the cleaning," he told the woman. "Both inside and out."

"Anytime, John," said Charlene. The blonde sat up in the tub, her eyes suddenly full of concern. "Be careful. That's a rough bunch you're riding with."

"I'll be all right," he assured her. "I can be just as ornery as they are, if need be."

"Still, watch your back," she warned.

Slocum bent down and gave her a parting kiss, then left. As he stepped out onto the landing, he saw that Flanders had a game of blackjack going. Slocum figured he had nothing better to do in the hours until Hicks gathered them for their nocturnal duties, so he descended the staircase, ready to try his hand at the game. If Lady Luck was as favorable toward him as the lady he had just left in the bathtub upstairs, he might just end up winning himself a dollar or two.

15

The call for their nightride came later that evening, well past eleven o'clock. Up until then, Slocum had been playing cards with one eye on the pasteboards and the other on the clock at the head of the upstairs landing. The contentment he had felt after his bath with Charlene had already worn off. Now an underlying nervousness crept beneath the Georgian's emotionless exterior. He recalled what Hicks had said earlier about how his rifle again might be needed, and all he could think about was who he might be forced to level his sights on. Would it be some farmer he hadn't yet come across? Or would it be someone he knew? Perhaps George Kelly or Will Sutherland?

The ball of nerves in his stomach clinched when Guthrie appeared through the doorway like always. "It's time," he whispered to Hicks, who sat directly across from Slocum at Flanders's felt-topped gambling table. The big Missourian simply nodded, laid his cards facedown, and pushed back his chair. The others followed their leader's example. Slocum did the same, although he would have much preferred sitting right where he was and spending the remainder of the night gambling. But, unfortunately, that was not an option for the dark-haired Southerner.

After joining with the others outside and making their silent journey to the livery stable, the twelve performed the same ritual they did every night. They dressed in their

113

black garb, checked their weapons, then saddled and mounted the horses that waited, well rested and fresh, in the corral out back.

When Hicks set off toward the east, Slocum was certain that they would be paying George Kelly a visit that night. He began to visualize the confrontation that might take place and knew that events would likely be much worse for the farmer than they had been during the night when he had stayed in the hayloft of Kelly's barn. The degree of violence had only seemed to escalate since Slocum joined the ranks of the nightriders and he felt as if this ride had the potential for becoming the bloodiest yet. Horrid scenes played through Slocum's mind: the cold-blooded lynching of Kelly and the brutal rape of Prissy by the half-drunk members of the midnight gang. He knew that if it came down to either, he would have no other choice than to abandon his plans and try to gun down as many of the nightriders as he could. He didn't cherish the thought of it. Eleven against one were lousy odds to buck, but then most of the men in the Judge's outfit weren't half as proficient with a six-shooter or a rifle as he was.

Halfway along the trail, Hicks reined his stallion due south. Slocum breathed a sigh of relief at the change of direction. It was clear to see that the Kelly farm wasn't their destination after all. Obviously, there was another farm within riding distance of Tyler's Crossing that they hadn't yet paid a visit to. Slocum asked no questions, however. He simply followed the others as they pushed their mounts into a steady gallop across the moonlit plains of central Kansas.

They rode for a solid hour. When they reached the winding channel of Smoky Hill River, they made a sudden turn, following the waterway westward. They left the river a half hour later and again changed direction. This time they rode northward. At first, Slocum wondered if Hicks had somehow become lost, but there seemed to be some sort of twisted logic to his rambling ride. Slocum gradually began to grow suspicious. It was almost as if Hicks was leading them to some place they knew, but was traveling a confusing route in order to keep them in the dark until they arrived.

They rode through a scrubby stand of pine and cedar, then emerged onto a stretch of flat pastureland. On the far side of the field, Slocum saw the moon-etched structures of a modest farm. No lights shone from the windows of the farmhouse. In fact, for all outward appearances, the place seemed completely deserted. But then Slocum recalled that the Jackson and Sutherland farms had also held the same deceptive look of utter desolation at first glance.

Without hesitation, Hicks led his nightriders onto the property. The horses and their equally dark riders flashed past ramshackle outbuildings and made a semicircle around the farmhouse. A mass of clouds had moved over the moon as they made their approach and hardly anything could be seen in the pitch-darkness. It was for that reason that Slocum failed to see one of the riders break away from the group and make a wide and silent sweep around the rear of the farmhouse.

Slocum reined his horse to a halt next to the towering structure of a windmill, then waited there, anticipating the boom of Hicks's voice demanding that the occupant show himself. But a minute passed and Hicks said nothing. Slocum looked around him. The nightriders sat silently in their saddles, facing the house. They seemed to have no questions concerning their leader's failure to act. Slocum tried to locate Hicks, but in the darkness he was unable to tell one rider from the next.

Just when Slocum began to get the feeling that something was wrong, the clouds moved westward, allowing the glow of the moon to fall earthward once again. Abruptly the details of the farm were revealed in the pale moonlight. The house and the surrounding buildings were weathered and close to collapse. The windows of the house were empty of glass and weeds grew heavy in the yard on all sides. A strange sense of déjà vu hit Slocum and he knew that he had been there before. Then he glanced down at the base of the windmill and saw the fallen blades of the rotor, each of them shorn from their iron hub by the force of a well-placed bullet.

Suddenly Slocum knew exactly where he was. The abandoned farm where he had proven his skill with a rifle to Luther Hicks.

He also knew that he was in the midst of a trap. But he had no time to defend himself. Just as he was reaching down to shuck his Winchester from the saddle boot, he heard the soft approach of a horse behind him. He tried to twist his head, but just as he did, the butt of a Dragoon pistol struck him heavily behind the left ear.

As he fell from his saddle and plunged into unconsciousness, he caught a fleeting glimpse of Luther Hicks sitting atop his coal-black stallion, his gray eyes twinkling cruelly over the black scarf that masked his lower face.

When Slocum finally came to, he found himself tied securely to one of the support poles of the old windmill. As he fought the heavy pain that thrummed within his skull, he felt the coolness of the night air against his skin. His shirt had been removed, revealing his scarred back to the gathering of black-clad riders who congregated around him.

"Wake up, John Slocum," came the gritty voice of Luther Hicks only a few feet away. "You've got a long night ahead of you."

Slocum turned his head and stared Hicks square in the eye. "Then you know who I am?"

Hicks laughed and nodded. "Oh, I didn't at first. I reckon that's because I thought you were long dead and rotting in your grave. I knew you kind of looked like John Slocum when you first arrived in Tyler's Crossing, but I didn't know it was you for sure for a couple of days. Not until we came out here and you worked some magic with that .44-40. I knew right then and there nobody on the face of earth could sniper-shoot like that . . . nobody but that reb Slocum I knew back when I rode for Quantrill and Bloody Bill. Then, last night, when you wounded Sutherland instead of outright killing him, I knew it was you, no questions asked." Hicks spat at the ground in disgust. "You still haven't lost that high and mighty side to you, even after all these years."

"I'm not so righteous," said Slocum. "I'm just not a murdering scoundrel like you are."

Hicks reared back, then kicked out forcefully. The toe of his boot caught Slocum in the side, just below the ribs. The Georgian grunted at the pain that burned through his abdomen. He felt his head being yanked back by the hair and the nasty heat of Hicks's breath against his face.

"You'd best keep your opinions to yourself," growled the leader of the nightriders. "Remember, I hated your frigging guts back during the war. I sure as hell don't feel any different about you now."

"I reckon you went and told Burke who I was," muttered Slocum.

"I didn't even have to," declared the bogus sheriff. "The Judge was sorting through some old wanted posters and came across one with a description fitting you perfectly. He wasn't none too happy that your crime happened to be judge-killing, either."

When the agony in his side began to subside, Slocum tested his bonds. Struggling was fruitless and escape next to impossible. Stout strands of rawhide bound his wrists together on the opposite side of the heavy timber. The rawhide would cut his flesh right down to the bone before it even came close to breaking.

"Oh, you ain't going nowhere, Slocum," said Hicks. "Not before you answer a few questions."

"You can go straight to hell, Hicks," said Slocum defiantly. "I'm not telling you a damned thing!"

Hicks sighed deeply. "Looks like you're just as mule-headed stubborn as ever, too." He stood up from his crouch and stepped back. "All right, boys. You've been gnawing at the bit to get your chance at him. Now you've got it."

Slocum sensed the nightriders closing in on him more than he saw it. They enclosed him like a suffocating blanket of pitch-black. First was the sound of harsh laughter and the stench of whiskey-tinged breath. Then the blows came. They hit him from all sides, slow at first, then quickening with the fury of being betrayed by one of their own. Fists punched and feet kicked, wracking his kneeling body with waves of uneasing agony. Soon, his blood flowed freely and his flesh became numb, so bruised was he. He knew that he sustained at least a couple of fractured ribs. He heard the brittle crack of them breaking as his rib cage was the target of someone's hard-toed riding boots.

Right when Slocum was sure that he would fall into unconsciousness again, Hicks called them off. "All right, boys! That's enough . . . for now." He crouched next to Slocum's battered form and seized his jaw roughly with one gloved hand. "Now, let's try it again. First of all, was that you who shot at us from the loft of Kelly's barn a couple of nights back?"

"I don't know what you're talking about," mumbled Slocum.

"That ain't the answer I wanted to hear," said Hicks. He drew his Dragoon from its holster and laid the long barrel forcefully against the top of Slocum's head. He pistol-whipped the tall Georgian several times before he finally returned the hogleg Colt back to his hip.

Slocum's head swam painfully and his eyes burned from the blood that ran from his scalp and down his face. He doubted the hatred he had felt for Luther Hicks and the other guerilla fighters when they had ambushed him years ago could have been any stronger than what he experienced right now.

"Here's another one for you," said Hicks. "What did you have in mind when you joined up with us? Were you intending to be some sort of frigging spy? And where did you go this morning after you left Tyler's Crossing?"

Slocum said nothing. He simply turned his head and spat a mouthful of blood squarely into the sheriff's face. Hicks stumbled back in surprise, looking as if he was a hairbreadth away from drawing his big horse pistol and emptying its cylinder into the defiant Southerner. But, before he could allow himself the pleasure of doing so, Hicks motioned to one of the nightriders. "Guthrie, get over here. And bring that bullwhip with you."

Guthrie stepped away from the others, slowly, his left hand letting the coil of the whip unfurl until its length snaked across the dusty earth. "How many lashes?" he asked of his boss.

Hicks shrugged as he took a cigar from his pocket and lit it. "I'll leave that up to you."

Guthrie laughed softly to himself. He walked up to Slocum and, crouching next to him, traced the pattern of old scars with his index finger, traveling his back from the nape of his neck to his lower spine. "Looks like you've had a taste of the whip before." Guthrie paused, took a twist of Kentucky tobacco from his pocket, and bit himself off a sizable chaw. "Bet it smarted like unholy hellfire. But

I'm betting it didn't hurt near as bad as I'm gonna make it hurt."

"Guthrie," whispered Slocum. "If you take that whip to me, I swear to God, I'll kill you. Somehow, somewhere, I'll make you pay dearly for it."

The lanky deputy with the pale eyes laughed coldly. "High talk for a man who's all broken up and half dead."

Slocum listened helplessly as Guthrie stood up and prepared to put his torturous skills to work. Guthrie stopped several yards away, turned to the side, then, gripping the haft of the bullwhip firmly in his left hand, sent the length of braided leather snapping outward with a loud crack.

The frayed tip of the bullwhip struck Slocum diagonally along the back, opening a shallow wound from left shoulder to right hip. It had been a long time since Slocum had felt the branding burn of whipcrack leather against his flesh. The sharp pain conjured images that he had thought to be long since forgotten. The dank shadows of a prison cell, the rattle of chains, and the low moans of men dying of festering wounds or the fever of sickness. And, most of all, there was the sound of the jailer's voice, counting off the fall of the whip a second before leather bit into flesh. Slocum remembered that as if it had happened only yesterday.

Again and again, Guthrie brandished his whip, bringing agony and blood, crisscrossing Slocum's back with fresh, new wounds. But Slocum gave the man no satisfaction. He uttered nothing more than a grunt or two. There was no screaming or begging for mercy. Slocum would have rather died than done that.

Finally, Guthrie's enthusiasm gave way to frustration. He tired of the lashing he was subjecting Slocum to and, walking up to the man, went a step further. He spat raw tobacco juice into Slocum's open wounds, hoping to elicit cries of agony that the whip failed to conjure. He was disappointed, however. Slocum endured the burn of the juice, gritting his teeth tightly and fighting to remain silent. He was determined to deny Guthrie the satisfaction of seeing him suffer.

"That's enough," said Hicks, motioning for Guthrie to return to his place among the others. He walked over and glared down at Slocum's bloody features. "You think you're one tough son of a bitch, don't you?" When Slocum refused to answer, Hicks moved in closer. "The Judge wanted me to kill you on account of your treason. But, if you ask me, a bullet in the brain pan would be too good for the likes of you. No, I think I'm gonna leave you tied out here. That Kansas sun gets mighty hot, particularly when the nearest water is a good mile or so away. I'd say, without food or water, you might last three or four days out here. That is, if the buzzards don't peck you to death first. They'd just as soon eat a man alive than dead."

"I won't forget this, Hicks," rasped Slocum hoarsely. "I promise you that."

Luther Hicks merely laughed and walked away. He climbed into his saddle, then stared down at the battered Georgian. "You should have left well enough alone, Slocum," was all he said before he reined his horse northward. As he spurred his stallion up the face of the ridge, the others did likewise. Soon they were gone from sight. A moment later even the pounding of their hooves faded into utter silence.

A cool night wind stirred up, whistling through the wooden struts of the windmill and engulfing Slocum's blood-bathed body in a cold chill. The pains that wracked his body eventually got the best of him and he felt himself begin to black out again.

Before he descended mercifully into oblivion, Slocum stoked the hatred deep down within him with thoughts of

the Judge and his marauding nightriders. His chances for
survival were slim at best, but Slocum knew that if anything
kept the spark of life burning within him, it would be his
desire for revenge.

16

The next four days were a living hell for John Slocum.

He awoke the morning after his brutal beating to find himself frying in the blazing Kansas sun. There was no shade to speak of beneath the lean framework of the old windmill, and if there had been, his bonds would have prevented him from acquiring its shelter. His wounds—the gashes across his back and the cuts on his scalp—seemed to have stopped bleeding, but that seemed like little consolation. He was stranded ten or fifteen miles from town, beaten half to death, with nothing to protect him from the fury of the sun and no food or water to sustain him.

The pistol-whipping that Luther Hicks had subjected him to had been a bad one. Sometimes he could feel his brain swelling inside his skull and the pain would grow so unbearable that he would black out completely. The first time that he passed out after his initial awakening, he figured that he must have lay in oblivion for several hours, for when he finally came to it was well past dusk. He jolted awake, confused by the darkness and the cool prairie wind that whistled around him. Moonlight etched the abandoned house and outbuildings, giving Slocum the eerie feeling of being helplessly stranded in the center of a desolate ghost town.

Although his mind was sluggish and his aching body yearned to return to the restful state of unconsciousness, Slocum fought to stay awake. He had spent enough time camped out on the trail to know that night was when most predators left their burrows and prowled the wilderness in search of food. He also knew that a steady campfire was what kept them at bay most of the time. There, lashed to the windmill without the benefit of such a fire, Slocum felt vulnerable and utterly defenseless. He could hear the distinct sounds of coyotes and foxes skittering through the thicket that grew heavily around the abandoned farm, and he wondered if they had smelled the scent of his blood. He was also painfully aware that rattlesnakes had a tendency to seek warmth from a sleeping body. Slocum despised sidewinders and he wasn't about to let one use his unconscious form as its makeshift bedroll.

Slocum managed to stay awake until dawn. Then, exhausted from the effort, he drifted off to sleep once again, cursing himself for getting mixed up in such troublesome business in the first place.

The second day of Slocum's imprisonment started upon his awakening at high noon. The Kansas sun hung like a flaming gold piece in the vast, cloudless sky. His skin began to change from a healthy bronze to a deep, sunburned red. His throat became dry and parched. He felt his bodily fluids begin to seep away in his sweat and he yearned for a drink of cool water. But he was without luck. Luther Hicks and the others had left him with no canteen, nor any source of food. An old well covered over with boards stood fifty feet away, but it might as well have been fifty miles. Besides, from the desolation of the farmstead, Slocum judged that the well was probably tainted and its water undrinkable.

The only thing that Slocum allowed to occupy his mind that day was his hatred for Luther Hicks and his band of cutthroat nightriders. Anyone with a shred of decency would have put a bullet in his brain and ended his torment before it could have reached such heights. But that had been the whole point of Slocum's abandonment. Hicks and the others had wanted to teach him a lesson for deceiving them. Staking him in the blazing sun without food or water was the worse torture a man could face. Slocum would have rather gone to hell and wrestled Satan himself than been subjected to fighting the elements . . . a fight that would eventually prove to be a losing battle.

As Slocum drifted back into unconsciousness toward the end of the day, he let thoughts of Judge Burke and Luther Hicks remain foremost in his mind. He refused to forget them or what they had done to him. He also wondered what they were up to, and if they had gone over the line of terrorizing the local farmers and actually murdered one of the defiant sodbusters yet.

The third day turned out to be much worse than the two previous days. Slocum's skin began to peel beneath the blistering heat of the prairie sun and he felt himself begin to dry up like the husk of some long-dead insect. He also began to feel the pangs of hunger and its weakening effects. His stomach rumbled and rolled, demanding sustenance. He was unable to provide for that demand, however. His wrists were still firmly bound by the cords of sturdy rawhide, and even if he had access to his immediate surroundings, there would have been nothing edible within reach. All that lay within six feet of him was earth, rock, and a few sun-scorched weeds. Every now and then, an insect would dart across the earth or scramble up one of the support beams of the windmill, but Slocum knew that he would rather die than resort to eating bugs.

As the sun began to set and the long shadows of evening stretched around him, Slocum pushed his obsessive hatred of the Judge and the nightriders out of his mind and turned to more comforting thoughts. He thought of Prissy Kelly and

Charlene, the saloon girl. He played the moments of pleasure they had shared over and over in his feverish mind, drawing some small amount of comfort from those sensual scenarios. He thought of the darkness of the hayloft, the softness of the hotel bed, and the soothing water of Charlene's bathtub. He wondered if either one of the women missed him or wondered what had become of him. Slocum finally decided that neither woman gave a damn about him. Not that he really expected them to. It was the destiny of a drifter like himself to be lonely and without the ties that a wife and family would bring him. Slocum enjoyed his freedom, but too many times that freedom had led him to trouble. This time his wandering had nearly gotten him killed and he wasn't sure that it wouldn't still succeed, if something drastic didn't happen before long.

Slocum began to hallucinate on the fourth day.

The combination of heat, hunger, thirst, and the severity of his wounds began to play tricks on Slocum's mind. It was small things at first. He would be certain that he heard someone's voice or the sound of a horse's hooves thundering over the distant ridge, but they all seemed to be figments of his imagination. Then, toward noon, when the sun reached its hottest peak, Slocum began to see things. He drifted in and out of consciousness, each awakening subjecting him to some new horror. Once he awoke to find himself surrounded by a dozen ebony-clad nightriders perched atop coal-black stallions. Their pistols and shotguns were cocked and aimed straight at him. Just as the hammers fell and Slocum was sure that he was about to be torn apart by bullets and buckshot, the dark forms shimmered in the hot air and vanished.

As the afternoon drew on, Slocum was haunted by his past. He awoke one time to find himself back amid the thunder and death of the War Between the States. He was at Gettysburg again, up on Little Round Top, firing upon the Union lines as Pickett's Division made its charge. Then he was on the battlefield after the fight. He smelled the stench of death, saw the bobbing of lanterns in the darkness, and heard the moans of injured and dying men. But this time Slocum found himself among the wounded. He sat against the base of a tree splintered and scarred by minié balls and grapeshot, waiting for someone to help him. When someone finally came, they ignored his protests and dumped him into a mass grave stacked six deep with the bodies of his Confederate brethren. As shovelfuls of earth covered him, sealing him into eternal darkness, he caught a glimpse of the face of the soldier who lay on top of him and, in horror, saw that it belonged to his brother Robert.

As the sun began to set and Slocum encountered one torturous tableau after another, one sight in the Kansas sky remained constant. Buzzards flew in wide, lazy circles above the farmstead. Slocum knew that they were patiently waiting for him to give up the ghost and die. But he declared that he wouldn't give them the convenience of an easy meal. Every time they swooped uncomfortably close, Slocum would yell to the high heavens, driving them away.

He knew, however, that he wouldn't be able to keep them at bay much longer. The following day they would grow bolder, while he grew weaker. Soon they would have their bellyful of flesh, whether he liked it or not.

That night, Slocum awoke to the sound of something moving through the thicket. Despite his grogginess, he grew alert. He stared across the moonlit farmstead and strained his ears. He heard voices on the other side of the old farmhouse and detected the dim glow of a light nearby.

Slocum crouched there helplessly as he heard steady foot-falls approaching from his blind side. He wished he had his

Colt Navy with him, but knew that it would have done him no good, not with his hands tied so securely. He waited anxiously, wondering if maybe he was in the throes of another mirage. Or perhaps it was Hicks, who had returned days later to finish up the job.

A moment later Slocum found out that it was no hallucination haunting him. Someone held a coal-oil lantern over him as they studied his bruised and battered form. "Lord Almighty!" whispered a man's voice. It was apparent that Slocum was the last thing on earth the stranger expected to find during his nocturnal visit to the abandoned farmstead.

Slocum lifted his head and attempted to speak. His words came out sounding more like a hoarse croak than anything else. "Who are you?"

The stranger knelt beside the injured man, and as the lamplight played across his face, Slocum discovered that he was really no stranger at all. The dark-skinned features of Elias Jackson stared down at him. He expected to see compassion in the man's eyes, but all that he could detect was guarded suspicion. He wondered why until Jackson pointed at his black britches and riding boots.

"Are you one of 'em?" asked Jackson angrily. "Are you one of those bastards that nearly hung me the other night?"

"I rode with them," said Slocum truthfully. "But not for the reason you think. I was hoping to stop them . . . then they found me out."

Elias Jackson stared hard into Slocum's eyes, as if searching the depths of his very soul. Then his expression of hatred began to slip away. "Heaven only knows why, but I do declare that I believe you."

Relief flooded Slocum as Elias reached out and, with a knife, cut away his rawhide bonds. He fell onto his back with a groan, his head swimming. He stared up and saw Jackson's wife and children draw near, eyeing him with fear. "He ain't gonna hurt us none," Elias told them. "He's too close to the grave to harm anyone."

Assured of his helplessness, Jackson's wife knelt next to Slocum and cradled his head in her hands. He felt something press against his lips and suddenly cool water was trickling past his parched lips and down his swollen throat. Slocum coughed and sputtered at first, then drank slowly from the canteen. The water hurt like hell at first, his gullet was so raw, but eventually the sting went away and the liquid began to soothe him.

The black farmer and his family gently carried Slocum to the rickety porch of the deserted farmhouse. As they laid him down, Slocum felt that familiar feeling of dark disorientation begin to overtake him and he knew that he was on the verge of blacking out again. He stared up at the farmer and uttered a single name, hoping that his urgency would convey the intended message.

"Prissy," he rasped in scarcely a whisper. "Prissy Kelly."

As Slocum's vision dimmed and he again drifted into unconsciousness, he saw the expression in Jackson's eyes turn from puzzlement to understanding. Slocum lay back and let himself go, hoping to God that the farmer would do the right thing and deliver him to the only place in Tyler's Crossing where Slocum felt he would be relatively safe.

17

The next time that Slocum opened his eyes, he found himself in surroundings completely opposite from the burning prairie where he had been unwillingly confined for the better part of a week.

As the veil of unconsciousness lifted from his mind, he discovered himself in cool darkness. The rich, dank odor of raw earth lingered heavily in his nostrils, and for a panicky second, Slocum recalled his feverish hallucination of being buried alive. But as he reached down and felt the soft material of a patchwork quilt draped across the lower half of his unclothed body, he knew that he lay not in a grave, but on the earthen floor beneath some sort of building. With no small amount of pain and effort, Slocum raised himself to his elbows and then reached upward with one outstretched hand. Just as he had thought. The tips of his fingers brushed against the low-hanging rafters of a house's crawl space.

At that moment the squeal of unoiled hinges echoed from the far side of the cramped area and dim light filtered in from an upper floor. Slocum looked over and was relieved to see Prissy Kelly making her way down a short stairway into the dark subchamber. She glared disapprovingly at him when she saw him sitting halfway up.

"None of that now," she said, rushing to his side and easing him down. "Lay back down this very minute!"

Slocum did as she said. His head felt heavier than a blacksmith's anvil and his eyes were playing tricks on him, causing him to see double. "Where am I?"

"In our root cellar," said Prissy. "Elias Jackson brought you here three days ago."

"Three days!" declared Slocum. "Has it been that long?"

"Yes, it has," Prissy told him. "You've been out of your head since Sunday." She reached out and felt his forehead. Her palm felt cool and comforting against Slocum's sun-blistered skin. "Good. It seems that your fever has broken."

"I reckon I owe you a debt of thanks for taking me in and nursing me like you have," said Slocum.

Prissy's lovely blue eyes hardened a bit. "You'd best save your thanks for my father," she told him flatly. "He was the one who agreed to hide you here in the cellar. To tell the God's honest truth, I had some grave misgivings about having anything else to do with you."

Slocum was surprised by Prissy's harsh words. "Why do you say that, Prissy?"

Anger showed clearly in the brunette's lovely face. "I reckon part of it's due to your leaving like you did. Not a good-bye nor a single word. You just up and left the following morning. I guess I expected something more, particularly after what we shared." Prissy shifted her eyes away, embarrassed at the memory of their passionate coupling in the hayloft of her papa's barn.

Slocum searched the woman's face and sensed that she had not told him the complete truth. "Is that all?"

Prissy hesitated at first, then turned back to Slocum, her eyes flashing. "No!" she hissed like an angry cat. "I also had my doubts about just whose side you were on." She reached to the ground beside her and grabbed up a pile of clothing. It was the black britches and riding boots that Slocum had worn on his last mission with Hicks and the nightriders.

"I can explain," said Slocum.

Prissy's eyes softened a degree. "There's no need to. Hinchburger rode out here the night before last and told Papa about what you were up to. But, still, the mere thought of you riding with those bastards . . . well, it's made me think twice about what sort of man you might be. For God's sake, John, one of the local farmers was shot and wounded last week!"

Slocum neglected to tell her that it had been him who was forced to shoot Will Sutherland. "Believe me, Prissy, I hated every damned minute of riding with that band. But, at the time, I thought it was the only chance I had of finding a way to stop Burke and his nightriders. I assume Hinchburger told you that I rode to the coach station southwest of here and had someone send a wire to the U.S. marshal in Fort Atkinson, asking for help."

Prissy's anger depleted even more. "Yes, he did mention that to Papa. But there's still one question I'd like answered. Why? You have no stake in this fight between the farmers and Hamilton Burke. You're just a saddle tramp passing through. Why would you go to so much trouble to help us?"

"Because I've had my fair share of head-butting with corrupt judges in the past, and out of the bunch, Burke takes the cake. The Judge offered me a job as one of his deputies, and when I refused, he threatened to throw me in the hoosegow if I didn't leave town. That went against my grain. He's using the same dirty tricks those thieving carpetbaggers used down South and I told myself that I wasn't going to let it happen again . . . not to decent folks like you and your pa. Well, Hicks and his men found out who I was and suspected what I was up to, and now look at me! What have I got to show for getting involved in such a sorry mess? I'm nearly half dead and you still have your suspicions about whether or not I'm one of Burke's nightriders!"

The brunette stared at the beaten and horsewhipped man, her heart softening at the sight of the abuse his body had been put through. "No, John," she said sweetly, her eyes growing softer with each moment. "Not any longer."

Abruptly the sound of footsteps on the wooden steps interrupted their conversation. They turned to see George Kelly making his way into the dank shadows of the root cellar.

"I thought I heard voices down here," said Kelly. "It's good to see you awake, John. You had poor Prissy worried half out of her mind for a couple of days there. We weren't sure if you were gonna make it." He knelt next to Slocum's pallet and eyed the injured man with concern. "How are you feeling, son? Or is that a foolish question to ask?"

"I feel a sight better than I did when I was lashed to that windmill out on the range," Slocum told him. "I'm sore as hell from head to toe and my vision is a bit shaky. But a little rest ought to fix me up in time."

"Are you hungry?" asked the farmer.

"I'm famished," Slocum told him.

George Kelly turned to his daughter. "Prissy, go on up to the kitchen and rustle up a mess of ham and eggs for this man."

"I sure will, Papa," said Prissy. She smiled warmly at Slocum, then ascended the steps to the house above. It wasn't long before they heard the clang of the woodstove door and the clatter of pans and skillets being prepared for cooking.

"You took a mighty big risk doing what you did," Kelly told the wounded drifter. "But I do appreciate it. All the other farmers hereabouts are obliged to you, too."

"You've talked to them since Jackson brought me here?" asked Slocum. "Do they know where I am?"

"Yes, but don't worry none," assured the elderly farmer. "They ain't about to cast you to the wolves. They hate the

Judge and his men with a passion. The Judge has been trying to take half of our property holdings away from us for nearly two months now, but he ain't had a bit of luck. All the other farmers are just as stubborn and mule-headed as I am."

"I just hope that marshal gets here before somebody gets killed," said Slocum. "The Judge is getting fed up with all the resistance he's been facing."

"I sure believe that," said Kelly. "Particularly where I'm concerned. He's been hounding me longer than the others . . . and not just because of my land either, the lousy son of a bitch."

"Prissy?" asked Slocum.

"Yes, that's the main thing he's after. I'll be damned if I know why. The way I hear it, that bullet that snapped his spine damaged him and he couldn't get it up if he wanted to. I think he's after Prissy mainly because she's the prettiest gal in these parts. To him, it'd be like winning a trophy if he had such a desirable woman for a wife."

"You're probably right about that," agreed Slocum. "Tell me something, Mr. Kelly. Have you heard anything concerning me? Any talk around town?"

"Well, the Judge and his men sure aren't saying anything," the farmer told him. "If they did, they'd be admitting that they were responsible for these nightrides against the farmers. But Hinchburger told me that he'd spoken to a whore at the saloon, and she told him that Burke and the others are privately searching for you. It seems that Luther Hicks rode out to that abandoned farm the other day and found you gone. And for some reason, that's made Hicks as nervous as a stud bull on gelding day."

"Let's just say that I knew Hicks before I even came to Tyler's Crossing," said Slocum, feeling some satisfaction at Hicks's jumpiness. "He did me wrong back then, just like he's done now, and he knows the next time we cross paths, I'll be out for blood."

"I understand." Kelly nodded. "I know a man like you feels easier having a gun close at hand, so I figured you might want to hang on to this." He brought an old cap-and-ball revolver from his waistband and laid it on the blanket next to Slocum's right hand. "It's just an old five-shot Colt Patterson, but it'll still kill a man just as dead as one of those newfangled Peacemakers will."

"Thanks for the loan of the gun," Slocum told him and he meant it.

"Well, I'd best get on back to my chores," said Kelly. "You just rest up and get back to healing." The old man sniffed and smiled. "Smells like Prissy will have those vittles down to you in no time." He reached out and shook Slocum's hand. "Again, I'm obliged to you for what you did. I'm just sorry that you almost got killed doing it."

"Let's just hope that U.S. marshal gets here before anyone else goes through the same hell I just went through," said Slocum.

"Amen to that, young man," agreed George Kelly. Then the old man turned and climbed back up the stairs to the ground floor of the modest farmhouse.

Slocum lay there, his anxiety eased quite a bit by the security he felt in the shelter of the Kellys' root cellar, as well the addition of the revolver nearby. The farmer hadn't said so, but Slocum knew that the Judge's men were out looking for him. They were determined to finish the job that Hicks had botched by leaving his old enemy stranded in the wilderness, and in time, their chances of doing so would grow more and more favorable.

Slocum felt like he had been trampled by a stampede of buffalo, but he knew that he must get back on his feet as fast as possible. If he didn't, Hicks and the other nightriders would eventually find him and kill him. And, afterward, they would punish George and Prissy Kelly for protecting him.

Of that, Slocum was absolutely sure.

18

During the next few days, Slocum spent his time recuperating.

His wounds still caused him much pain and were annoyingly slow in healing. His head and abdomen were bound with bed linen that Prissy had cut into strips, and beneath those dressings, his battered brain and cracked ribs mended slowly, changing from near agony to little more than a dull throbbing. The cuts and bruises inflicted by the fists and boots of the nightriders were healing nicely, as were the ugly marks that Guthrie's bullwhip had etched across his back. The night following Slocum's awakening, Elias Jackson and his family had made a secretive visit to the Kelly farm. Elias's wife, Nettie, had concocted a soothing poultice of herbs and river mud that had taken much of the sting from the deep gashes.

Plenty of rest and good food from Prissy's kitchen proved to speed up Slocum's recovery. As one day passed into another, he could feel his pain lessen, while his strength gradually increased. In the daytime, Prissy would sit by his makeshift bed in the root cellar, reading to him by lantern light. At night, Hinchburger or one of the neighboring farmers would stop by after dark and spend an hour or so in the company of Slocum and George Kelly, discussing the increase in the nightriders' activities or simply playing a few hands of cards. So far, no sign of the U.S. marshal from Fort Atkinson had been seen in the vicinity of Tyler's Crossing. Slocum began to wonder if his ride to the coach station had been in vain; if somehow the Judge had intercepted his message before it could reach the proper authorities. In any event, the hopes of the local farmers were beginning to flag considerably. And it was plain to see that Hamilton Burke was losing his patience. They knew if something wasn't done soon, the Judge would no longer be content with attempting to take away a percentage of their properties. Instead, he would try to wrestle away the entire ownership of their land, leaving them with absolutely nothing.

A week after he had been entrusted to the care of the Kellys, Slocum was spending a quiet afternoon in the darkness of the root cellar when he heard the sound of a horse-drawn carriage. He cocked his head and listened carefully as the buggy crossed the Kelly property and came to a halt next to the back porch of the farmhouse. Above him, Slocum could hear the drumming of Prissy's footsteps on the floorboards overhead as she crossed the kitchen to the back door.

"What do you want?" came Prissy's voice. Although it was muffled, Slocum could hear a definite edge in her usually cheerful tone.

"I was just in the neighborhood and thought I would stop and call on you, Miss Kelly," came the crisp reply.

Slocum bristled. He recognized the voice of Hamilton Burke instantly. He shook his bandaged head in wonder. The man had a hell of a nerve showing up at the Kelly farm after what he had been up to lately.

"The next time you go for a ride in the country, Judge, I'd prefer that you pass this place by," Prissy told him firmly. "You're not welcomed here."

"I'm sorry to hear you say that, my dear," said the Judge.

"Particularly since I came here solely with your best interest in mind."

"What do you mean?" Prissy's voice was guarded. Slocum could detect a mixture of suspicion and fear in the young woman's voice.

"I understand that some ruffians have been molesting you and your father lately," said the Judge. "A band of scoundrels clad in black."

Prissy laughed harshly. "More like puppets, I'd say."

Burke ignored her comment. "In any case, I'm deeply disturbed by your predicament. And being rather fond of you, Miss Kelly, I've decided to take it upon myself, as your potential benefactor, to put an end to your trouble."

"What are driving at?" asked Prissy.

"What I am driving at, Prissy, my dear, is a proposal of marriage," said the Judge. "Become my wife and, I assure you, those heathens will no longer pester you or your father."

Slocum felt his anger rise. He reached over and clenched the butt of the Colt Patterson. The gall of the man, actually proposing to Prissy on such dishonorable conditions. He had a mind to go upstairs and end the Judge's unlawful conquests once and for all, but Slocum knew that he would never make it. He was still weaker than water, and even if he did make it to the back porch, he had to contend with the annoying case of double vision the pistol whipping had inflicted upon him. He was normally a crack shot, but he was sure to lose his advantage due to the distortion the concussion had caused. He recalled the twin pepperbox pistols that the Judge carried in his vest pockets and knew that it would be best to stay put.

When Prissy finally found the power to speak, it seemed like she was just as outraged by the Judge's proposal as Slocum. "You must be joking," she said.

Burke's voice was cold and uncompromising. "No, Prissy,"

he told the farmer's daughter. "I am completely serious."

"Well, you'd best strike the notion from your mind," said Prissy in utter disgust. "I'd just as soon wed the Devil himself than spend one moment alone with a slimy snake like you!"

The Judge said nothing for a long moment. Slocum could picture the crippled Judge sitting in his fancy buggy, fuming at Prissy's insulting rejection. But when Burke spoke once again, there was no trace of anger in his voice. "I'm sorry to hear that, Miss Kelly. I was hoping that you would be more favorable toward my suggestion. In any case, I feel sorry for you and your father. If you refuse to give me your hand in marriage, I'm afraid there's nothing I can do to protect you from those godless nightriders. And from what I gather, they're becoming more bloodthirsty and prone toward violence with each passing night."

"As if you haven't had a hand in this business all along!" scoffed Prissy in anger. "Now I suggest you cut your visit short and get the hell off my father's land! And don't get any ideas about coming back. You're lucky Papa is out tending the fields. If he had heard your sickening proposal, he would have shot you dead!"

Burke laughed, but it was a cold, emotionless laugh. "You are quite a spirited woman, Prissy Kelly. I prefer that trait in a female." Slocum could picture the Judge smiling at Prissy with that oily, reptilian grin of his. "Don't think that I've taken your dismissal to heart. No, far from it. Hamilton Burke takes whatever he desires, no matter what steps must be taken to accomplish his goal. You would do good to remember that."

"I've heard enough," Prissy told him. "Now get out of here."

Slocum heard the horse and buggy make a sharp turn in the barnyard, then set off back down the trail toward town.

When the sound of the carriage had faded, Slocum called out, "Prissy . . . are you all right?"

"Yes," replied the woman from the room above, but from her tone of voice Slocum could tell that the Judge's visit had upset her.

A few minutes later Prissy made her way down the cellar steps. She carried a pan of warm water and a washrag. "You haven't had a decent bath since Jackson and his family first brought you here. I figured it was about time you had one."

"I agree," said Slocum. As she sat down on the earthen floor next to him, he reached out for the cloth and water.

"No, you just lay back and rest," Prissy reprimanded. "I'll do it for you, that is, if you're not too modest about letting me."

Slocum smiled. "No one's ever accused me of being that, Prissy."

Prissy returned the smile. She pulled down the quilt that covered Slocum, revealing his naked form. The bruises on his arms, torso, and legs were gradually fading, but they were still ugly to look at.

"I suppose you heard what happened upstairs," said Prissy. She dipped her rag in the water, soaped it up, and gently began to bath Slocum's head and shoulders.

"Yes, I did," said Slocum, scarcely biting back his anger. "The nerve of the bastard asking you such a question."

Prissy's bathing moved along Slocum's hairy chest and the lengths of his muscular arms. "Imagine me, married to someone such as him," she said. "He's responsible for putting Tyler's Crossing under lock and key, as well as terrorizing all the farmers hereabouts, my father included. I'd be crazy to accept a proposal of marriage from such a dishonest and deceitful man."

Slocum simply nodded. He lay back and closed his eyes. The feel of the wet rag against his flesh was comforting, as well as sensual. As Prissy began to bathe his feet and slowly progress up his legs to his knees and upper thighs, Slocum felt himself become aroused.

"No," continued Prissy. "I could never have such a man as a husband. Besides, he's a cripple. He could never pleasure me in the same way that a whole man could. Not the way you have, John."

The soapy rag suddenly left Slocum's legs, instead finding a much more tender and sensitive area. The man groaned aloud as the cloth massaged his testicles. His already aroused prick grew rigid beneath Prissy's maddening touch. Slocum looked up at the girl above him and saw that the same expression of growing lust lurked in Prissy's pretty blue eyes.

"I want you, Prissy," he said. "I want you bad. But I'm afraid I'm not in much shape to do the job right."

"No," agreed Prissy. "But I am." She reached around her back and began to unbutton her dress. She stood, letting the garment of flowered gingham fall around her feet. Slocum stared up at her naked body, relishing the smooth curves of her breasts and hips, the creamy paleness of her skin, and the darkness of her nipples and pubic thatch. She knelt upon his lower legs and, removing the pins from the bun of her hair, let her long trestles fall upon his genitals. The feel of her hair against him made Slocum shiver involuntarily.

"What about your father?" he asked her.

"Like I told Burke, he's out working his fields," said Prissy. "He won't be in until supper, and that's several hours away." She lifted her head, slung her long brown hair over her shoulders, then lowered her face to his crotch.

The feel of Prissy's lips against his manhood was indescribable. From their previous encounter, Slocum knew that Prissy wasn't as demure and frigid as most farm girls were, but still he was surprised by the wildness she now displayed. She took him into her mouth, her lips and tongue sending thrills of pleasure through his prick and clean up the base of his spine. He moaned and lay back, watching as her head bobbed up and down at a slow and steady pace.

Right when he was sure that he was on the verge of shooting his load, Prissy pulled away and grabbed the base of his cock, delaying his release. "Not so fast," she told him with a wicked smile. "I'm not finished yet."

Slocum knew what she had in mind. "Then, by all means, finish what you started," he suggested.

Prissy crawled up his legs until she squatted directly over his hips. She reached up and took hold of the support beam of the floor overhead, then lowered herself upon the man. Slocum slid into her wet pocket with no trouble at all.

Slocum reached up and cupped a pert breast in each hand as Prissy went to work. Her hips bucked and rolled as she rode the spike of Slocum's manhood. The ride didn't last for long, however. Feeling his sap begin to rise, Slocum ignored the soreness of his body and began to do his part, feeding it up to her. As they both came, Prissy lost her hold on the cellar rafter. She fell into Slocum's strong arms, shuddering and groaning, until the last spasms of ecstasy swept through her body and, eventually, faded away.

The man and woman shared a tender kiss, then Prissy rolled off her lover, a naughty smile on her lips. "Well, it seems like your injuries haven't hurt you none in that respect."

"No," replied Slocum. "I reckon that was the one part of my body that didn't get damaged."

They lay on the earthen floor of the root cellar, silently, side by side, until Prissy heard the chiming of three o'clock echo from a clock upstairs. Reluctantly she got up and dressed, then put her hair back up the best she could. "I hate to go, but I'd best get to cooking. If Papa comes in and finds supper late, he might suspect something."

Slocum nodded. "Go ahead. And thanks for the bath . . . and everything else."

Prissy grinned, her blue eyes flashing. "Believe me, John . . . it was my pleasure."

"But not yours entirely," he told her.

He watched as she took the pan and washrag, and climbed the steps to the kitchen above. As the cellar door closed and Slocum was again confined to darkness, he pulled the quilt back over him and lay back, his mind turning to serious thought. It had been a long time since he even considered making a life with a woman, but Prissy was the kind of lady who brought out such thoughts in a drifter such as himself. For years he had ridden the territories of the West, first driven there by the threat of arrest and conviction for the killing of a judge, a killing that had been wholly justified in his mind, but not in the mind of a federal government involved in a vengeful reconstruction of the rebellious South. Then, after the threat of immediate capture had waned, he simply drifted for the freedom of the open plains and the towering mountains. But every now and then he would grow weary of wandering and meet a woman like Prissy who put thoughts of settling down and raising a family back into his mind.

Of course, such domestic yearnings never lasted more than a short while. For some reason or another, he always found a reason for saddling his horse and moving on . . . whether it turned out to be a good reason or not.

19

That night, Slocum was awakened by the sound of gunfire.

He snapped awake, his heart pounding in his chest. After the Judge's visit to the Kelly farm earlier that day and his no-win proposition to Prissy, Slocum had half expected something to take place that night. And from the commotion that jolted him from his sleep, he knew that the nightriders were back in full force and prepared to do some real damage.

Slocum kicked off his blankets and, biting back the pain of his injuries, struggled into his britches and boots. Just as he grabbed up the old Colt revolver, the trapdoor opened above him with a squeal of rusty hinges. Slocum thumbed back the hammer and aimed at the form who appeared at the lighted portal. His vision was still distorted, so he wasn't sure who the intruder was at first glance.

"It's me!" said Prissy in a whisper. She was dressed only in her nightgown, but carried her father's Henry rifle in her right hand. Slocum made a move toward her, but she motioned him back. Prissy slammed the trapdoor shut behind her and secured it with an iron bolt that locked the entrance from underneath.

As she reached his side, Slocum could hear the drumming of boots on the floorboards above, as well as the crashing of furniture and the smashing of dishes and cookware. "Those damned nightriders are back with a vengeance!" the woman told him. "I expected as much, after I jilted Burke this afternoon."

They could hear several nightriders attempting to pry open the trapdoor overhead. "Where is your father?" he asked as Prissy helped him to his feet.

"The bastards got him!" she said, half fearful and half enraged. "They came in through his bedroom window and dragged him off into the night. I entered the room just as they'd taken him and was coming back through the window for me. Fortunately, Papa's rifle was still in the corner. I shot the first one and drove the others off." She cocked an ear and heard the racket of marauding men echo from the kitchen above. "Luckily, I made it down here before they gathered their nerve up again."

"How are we going to get out?" asked Slocum.

"There's a trapdoor on the far side of the cellar that leads to the outside," Prissy told him. "Papa uses it in the winter months to store firewood down here."

Together, they made their way through the pitch-darkness, until they reached the southern wall of the farmhouse's stone foundation. Double doors of sturdy oak were hidden behind a rick of split kindling. Slocum and Prissy dug their way past the jumble of firewood, then unclasped the doors and swung them open.

As they emerged into the night, they found chaos around them. The barn, the chicken coop, and the other outbuildings . . . all had been set aflame. Their burning structures lit up the dark Kansas sky. "Damn them!" cursed Prissy, nearly in tears. "Damn them for what they've done!"

Slocum was leading the distraught woman away from the house and toward the cover of the wheat fields fifty yards away when one of the nightriders emerged from around the corner of the farmhouse. "Hold it right there!" he warned, drawing a Star .44 from his hip.

Slocum lifted his own Colt without a second thought, but hesitated when he realized that he saw two of the man in the glow of the flames instead of merely one. He knew that he couldn't delay for long, however. He had to act now, or not act at all. He leveled his gun at the form nearest the corner of the house and fired, hoping that he had aimed at the right target. Fortunately, he had. His bullet found the center of the nightrider's chest, driving him hard to the ground. He made no effort to get back up.

"Come on," said Slocum. Prissy choked back her tears long enough to assist the wounded man across the barnyard, toward the dark wall of waist-high crops. Halfway there, a rider appeared around the side of the barn and charged them. "Allow me!" said Prissy. She lifted the Henry to her shoulder, levered a cartridge into the breech, and snapped off a single shot. The slug screamed past the head of the black stallion and caught its rider squarely in the throat. Gagging, the man slipped from the saddle, but his left foot failed to clear its stirrup. The frightened horse bounded off into the darkness, dragging its dying rider with it.

Finally, they reached the shelter of the wheat field. As they crouched amid the dense crop, Slocum and Prissy watched helplessly as the nightriders left the farmhouse, then set it on fire with torches. Prissy sobbed quietly as her home burned quickly, the flames consuming the dry wood and cedar shingles almost hungrily. Slocum held her tightly, turning her face toward his shoulder so she could not see the devastation of the Kelly farm.

He watched as the nightriders cast their torches aside and remounted. It was only then that he noticed several other men on horses near the barbed-wire corral. They were clad in nightclothes, their hands tied securely to the horns of their saddles, and their heads totally covered by flour sacks. Slocum could only guess at their identities, but he had a good idea that George Kelly was among them.

"We're heading on!" roared the voice of Luther Hicks. The leader of the nightriders reined his horse next to the prisoners, then pointed toward a couple of his associates. "McGraw, you and Tipton stay behind. Search the place and try to find that girl if you can. The Judge will have our hides for letting her slip through our fingers!"

As Hicks and the other nightriders herded the bound riders toward the trail, Tipton and McGraw drew their guns and started, on foot, across the barnyard, watching for some sign of the girl. Slocum knew they would come across his and Prissy's footprints in the dusty earth before long and he would end up having to take on two seasoned gunmen at one time. And considering his faulty vision, he wasn't so sure that he could do that successfully.

Slocum never got the chance to find out. Before the two nightriders were halfway across the dirt yard, he heard the rustle of wheat sound behind him. Startled, Slocum swung around, lifting the Patterson into line. He relaxed his grip and let the barrel sag when he spotted a dark and familiar face staring back at him from the concealment of the high rushes.

"It's just me, Mr. John," said Elias Jackson. "You'd best come along. I'll see that you and Miss Prissy get to somewhere safe."

Slocum didn't argue. He and Elias led the weeping woman through the acres of summer wheat, away from the flaming pire that had once been her homestead. As the fields gave way to open range, they reached a twisted cedar with two animals tethered to the trunk. One was a fine gelding, while the other was an aged, sway-backed plow mule.

Elias helped Slocum and Prissy onto the back of the horse, then climbed atop the mule, despite the protest of the stubborn creature. "Stick close to me," he told Slocum. "We've got a ways to ride."

Slocum nodded. Taking the gelding's reins, he followed the black farmer southward across the dark plains. He glanced back over his shoulder only once. The Kelly farm was no more than fire, billowing smoke, and charred timbers. "Don't worry, Prissy," he whispered in the grieving woman's ear. "We'll make them pay. I swear to God, we will."

It was daybreak before they reached their destination.

The scrubby vegetation and sun-browned grass of the open plains ended as they approached the Smoky Hill River, giving way to tall oaks and cedars, as well as thick stands of greenery. After riding a mile or so along the muddy channel, they came to a sharp bend in the river. Camped on its northern bank were several families. As the rode into camp and dismounted, Slocum saw that there were no men among the gathering, only women and children.

As the group approached the new arrivals, their eyes desperate and full of worry, Slocum looked at the black farmer, seeing the same expression on his dark face. "What's going on here, Jackson? Who are these people?"

"Let's get us some coffee and I'll tell you," said Elias.

Slocum and Prissy followed the man to a cookfire beneath a curved oak. Soon, tin cups were filled with hot coffee, and after a few sips, Jackson began to speak. "Those nightriders had their work cut out for them last night. They started just after dusk, riding from farm to farm, taking the head of each household and then setting the houses and barns on fire. The Kelly farm was the last place they visited and George was the last one of the bunch to be captured."

Prissy leaned over and spoke to Slocum in a low voice. "I recognize most of these women and young'uns. They're the families of the local farmers. That's Marjory Sutherland over yonder, as well as Hazel Canton and her brood, and Sarah Pike and her four children."

"But what was the point of the nightriders abducting your father and the rest of the farmers?" asked Slocum, although the reason was slowly becoming clear in the back of his mind.

"What other point could there be?" said Elias. "Judge Burke has gotten sick and tired of us sodbusters resisting his demands. He's decided that half of our land ain't nearly enough anymore. Now he wants it all. He's captured the other farmers and will probably threaten and torture them until they finally break down and sign over their deeds to the bastard." Jackson grinned broadly. "They'd have gotten me, too, but after I deserted my farm, they didn't know where to look."

"Any idea where they've taken the men?" asked Prissy.

"I think so," said Jackson. "The most likely place would be the old Woodard place."

Prissy seemed surprised. "You mean the farm where you found John?"

"That's right," said the Negro farmer. "After the nightriders torched your papa's farm, that was the direction they were headed."

"I've heard that criminals always return to the scene of the crime," said Slocum, angrily recalling his brutal beating and the hellacious days that followed. "I reckon they think that's one place nobody'll bother looking."

"Well, they're dead wrong," declared Elias. " 'Cause I'm planning on riding there tonight and do my best to get them out of there. I'm sick of being scared of the Judge and his men. I'm ready to face up to them now."

"Then I'll be going with you," said Slocum.

"I don't think you're in any shape to be taking on those hired guns," Prissy reprimanded. "You can't even see straight."

"Maybe I can do something about that," said Jackson's wife. "Are you willing to let me work my magic on you again, Mr. Smith?"

Slocum recalled the quickness with which the poultice had healed the whip marks on his back. "Sure. Go ahead."

Nettie Jackson left and returned briefly with the tools of her doctoring. Slocum sat against the trunk of the oak while she rubbed a smelly salve into his eyes, then covered them with damp moss from the riverbank. She held the strange concoction in place with a bandanna.

"Now what?" asked Slocum. He felt useless sitting there, unable to see what was taking place around him.

"I have to ride out and meet someone," said Elias Jackson. "We'll be back here by nightfall. Hopefully you'll be ready to ride by then."

"But who are you meeting?" asked Slocum.

"A mutual friend," was all that Jackson would tell him before he mounted the gelding and headed north.

"You just lay back and rest up," Nettie told him. "Miss Prissy, I'd be obliged if you'd help me put this oil on him. It'll help take the soreness out of his arms and legs."

Prissy agreed, and together, the two women began to apply a thin oil to Slocum's bruised muscles. "What the hell is that?" asked Slocum. "It stinks worse than the other stuff."

"Stop your complaining," Prissy told him. "Just take a nap and let us do our work."

The escape from the Kelly farm and the long ride to the riverbank had taken a lot out of Slocum, so he complied to Prissy's request. Soon, he was fast asleep, the soothing touch of the women's hands and the gentle rush of the river lulling him into slumber.

Slocum awoke several hours later to the sound of horses approaching from the north.

He reached to the ground next to him for the Colt Patterson, his other hand on the verge of ripping the bandanna and its healing poultice away. Before he could, though, Prissy reached out and stopped him. "It's only Elias and his friend," she told him.

Slocum listened as the two men entered the camp and then dismounted, tying their horses to a stand of brush nearby. The crackling of the campfire and the slow sizzle of beans and bacon in an iron kettle didn't mask their footsteps as they approached the base of the huge oak tree.

The Georgian's apprehension eased some when a strong, work-callused hand reached out and grabbed Slocum's own. "How the hell are you doing, John?" rumbled a deep, gravelly voice in his ears.

A smile split Slocum's battered face. "Hinchburger! So you're the mutual friend!"

"That's right," said the burly liveryman. "I reckon Elias has told you what the Judge has been up to?"

"He has," said Slocum. "Are they being held where Jackson thought?"

"Yes, they're at the same place they ambushed you and left you to rot," said Hinchburger. "Believe me, John, I'd sure have come out and helped you. But I had no idea what had become of you until Elias found you tied to that windmill."

Being unable to see who he was talking to irritated Slocum. "Can I take this mess off my eyes now?" he asked.

"Not yet," came the voice of Nettie Jackson next to the fire. "Just a little while longer. You eat a bite now. All of you."

Plates of beans and cornpone were dished up and passed around. Everyone was quiet as they ate, each thinking of the danger their loved ones were in and what they could do to rescue them. After the food, coffee was served. As Slocum drank the strong brew, he was relieved to feel the black woman's able hands begin to untie the bandanna. "Now let's see if I've done you some good," she said.

When Nettie lifted the poultice from his eyes and wiped the excess of the salve away, Slocum squinted against the flames of the campfire. It was already late evening, but the firelit forms of those around the fire could be seen. For a moment, his vision remained as before, doubled and distorted. Then it began to clear. It wasn't long before his sight was as crisp and clear as it had ever been.

"Someone hand me a gun," said Slocum. "I want to make sure I can shoot as well as I can see."

Hinchburger took a pistol from his coat pocket and tossed it to him. "There you go. And I'm betting it's a gun you're accustomed to handling, too."

Slocum was surprised to find himself holding his old Colt Navy revolver. "But where did you get it?"

"Can you believe that one of Hicks's men sold it to me?" The blacksmith laughed. "He was in need of gambling money, so I bought it from him for a couple of dollars. I'm just glad it's back in the right hands."

"So am I," replied Slocum. He climbed to his feet, amazed at how easily he now moved. Most of the soreness and stiffness was gone from his arms and legs, thanks to the miracle oil that Jackson's wife had concocted. He raised the revolver at arm's length and aimed it toward the river. A large clump of driftwood stood on a sandbar in the center of the water, barely illuminated by the flames of their campfire. He set his sights, cocked back the hammer, and fired. The bullet found its mark, shearing a jagged limb from the log.

He turned back toward the others. "All right, I'm ready."

"Then let's ride," suggested Hinchburger. He tossed the grounds of his coffee cup into the fire, then stood. He held a big, double-barreled ten-gauge in his work-hardened hands.

Marjory Sutherland walked over to Slocum, handing him a shirt and hat. "Take these, Mr. Smith. They're my husband's. There's no need for you leaving here half naked."

Slocum took the clothing. "I'm obliged to you, ma'am."

"Just bring back my Will," she told him. "That's all I ask."

"I'll sure do my best," he assured her.

Slocum carefully slipped the shirt over his wounded chest and back. Prissy came over and began to help him button it up. "The same goes for me, John," she said, her eyes pleading. "Please bring my father back to me."

"Don't worry," he said. "I will."

Prissy walked over to the base of the tree and brought back her father's brass-framed rifle. "Here. I want you to take the Henry."

"Only if you'll keep your papa's pistol," said Slocum. He pressed the .36-caliber Patterson into her dainty palm. "We'll be back as soon as possible."

"We'll pray for you," said one of the farmers' wives.

Slocum accompanied Hinchburger and Jackson to where the horses were tied. He was pleased to find that Hinchburger had possessed the forethought to bring his spotted gelding. Slocum ran a comforting hand along the horse's neck, then swung into the saddle. He stuck the Henry rifle into the boot that usually held his Winchester, then following Jackson's lead, headed westward toward the old Woodard farm.

20

An hour later Slocum, Hinchburger, and Jackson reined their horses to a halt on top of the ridge north of the abandoned farm. They swung down from their saddles and tethered the animals to a clump of thistle. Then the three men crept to the edge of the ridge and studied the neglected structures below.

All seemed like dark, unoccupied hulls except for the farmhouse and the barn. The faint glow of coal-oil lamps could be detected through the broken windows and around the edges of the doors. Slocum strained his ears for sound and, after a moment, heard noises drift up from the scrubby valley. A cry of pain echoed from the vicinity of the farmhouse, accompanied by the snickering of cruel laughter. The ugly sounds stoked Slocum's anger. He recalled hearing similar laughter while he was being kicked and pummeled by Hicks's nightriders no more than a hundred yards away.

They checked their guns, then made their way silently off the ridge toward the farmstead below. As they emerged from the brush next to the windmill and started across the scrubby yard, they could also hear laughter coming from the tall structure of the barn. From the sounds of revelry they knew that the nightriders who occupied the barn were half drunk on cheap whiskey.

Slocum motioned to his friends to stay put for a moment, then quietly mounted the front porch of the farmhouse. He eased toward a window of the front room and took a quick peek through the busted panes. Three nightriders were sitting around a table in the center of the room. Also sitting there, bound securely to a chair with heavy rope, was George Kelly. The flour sack that had once covered the head of the elderly farmer was gone now. Slocum winced at the sight of the battering Kelly's face had been subjected to. His left eye was swollen shut and he was bleeding profusely from the nose and mouth. As Slocum stood there watching, he saw one of the black-clad riders rise from his chair and strike the old man with the barrel of a Remington pistol. An ugly gash opened across Kelly's brow and blood began to flow into the farmer's uninjured eye.

"We've been at this for an hour now, Kelly," growled the nightrider. "Why don't you stop being so damned stubborn. If you sign this paper on the table, we'll put an end to this right here and now, and take you back out to the barn."

George Kelly glared at his captor and spat a glob of bloody spittle into the nightrider's masked face. "It'll be a cold day in hell before I sign over my land to the likes of you and that son of a bitch Burke."

The rider shook his head in frustration. "All right, Kelly. I gave you a fair chance. Looks like I'm gonna have to turn this matter over to my buddy over yonder."

Slocum shifted his gaze from the center of the room to the crackling hearth at the left end of the room. A nightrider crouched next to the fireplace, fiddling with something, turning the long object slowly in the flames. When the man stood up, Slocum was shocked to see that the man held a branding iron. The end of the iron glowed bright red. Slocum had ridden enough cattle drives to know what a brand could do to the tough hide of a cow, let alone the fragile flesh of a man.

He slipped back off the porch and rejoined Hinchburger and Jackson. "You fellows take the barn," he said. "I'll take the house."

They nodded in understanding, then slipped off into the darkness. Slocum watched until the night swallowed them, then crept around the side of the abandoned farmhouse. When he reached the back door, he found it unlocked and standing halfway open on its rusty hinges. He entered the cluttered kitchen and made his way silently across the room, praying that he didn't step on any squeaky boards. Fortunately, he didn't. He reached the hallway that crossed over to the front room without making any noise at all.

Slocum stood there in the shadows of the alcove and watched as the nightrider started toward George Kelly with the branding iron in his hand. From the gleam of pure sadism in the outlaw's eyes, Slocum knew that he intended to use it, too. The tall Georgian wasn't sure if Hinchburger and Jackson had reached the barn yet, but he knew he couldn't wait any longer. He had to act now, or Kelly would end up permanently disfigured or dead.

As the nightrider stopped before the bound man and twirled the glowing head of the brand no more than six inches from Kelly's face, Slocum made his move. He slipped the Colt Navy from the waistband of his britches and stepped into the room.

The other two nightriders saw him before the third did. Slocum let them rise from their chairs, even let them get their hands on the butts of their revolvers, before he fired. His aim proved to be as true as it ever had been. One bullet punched through the center of one nightrider's forehead, while another opened a hole in the other outlaw's chest, just above his heart.

As his friends fell dead around him, the third nightrider tossed the branding iron away and went for his own pistol.

Slocum thumbed back the Navy's hammer and snapped off a shot. The slug tunneled through the nightrider's stomach, driving him backward. The man tripped over the stone lip of the hearth and fell, kicking and screaming, into the mouth of the fireplace. As flames engulfed him, Slocum considered letting the outlaw burn to death. Then his basic decency made him think better of it and he fired a single shot, putting the wailing man out of his misery.

George Kelly squinted through the blood in his eyes. "John? Is that you?"

"It's me," said Slocum. He picked the hot iron off the floor and carefully began to burn away Kelly's ropes. "I'll have you loose in a moment."

As Slocum went to work, he could hear the crack of gunfire echo from the direction of the barn.

Hinchburger and Elias Jackson were standing outside the barn doors, guns cocked and ready, when the first report of Slocum's gun boomed from the farmhouse behind them. They looked at one another, then put their brawny shoulders to the big door and knocked it open.

As they stepped into the barn, they took in the surroundings of the huge structure, which was illuminated only by a couple of kerosene lanterns. In the center of the barn's earthen floor sat half a dozen men, bound with sturdy rope and wearing flour sacks over their heads. Standing around the captive farmers were five nightriders. Two were reaching for rifles and shotguns, while the other three were already starting toward the general direction of the gunfire outside.

Hinchburger reacted first. He leveled his ten-gauge from the hip and squeezed both triggers. The blast from the scattergun caught the three closest to the door. A bee swarm of double-aught buckshot engulfed them, peppering their heads and upper chests. Two died instantly, while the third fell to his back, mortally wounded but still alive. The liveryman ducked behind the wooden partition of a stall, just as the gunman fired a couple of shots at him. He crouched low as splinters spun about his head, quickly breaking open the breech of the shotgun and reloading with fresh shells. He then rolled back into the open, aimed his scattergun at the wounded man, and unleashed a single barrel. It did the trick and the nightrider went down, unable to rise a second time.

While the liveryman concentrated on his three, Elias Jackson centered his attention on the two who were busily arming themselves. He raised an old Spencer repeating rifle to his shoulder and drew a bead on a burly nightrider toting a Parker twelve-gauge. He fired once, spinning the big man around on his heels. Jackson cocked the lever and squeezed the trigger again. The second slug dug deeply into the outlaw's chest, ripping through the muscle of his heart. The nightrider fell flat on his face, dead before he hit the ground.

The second nightrider jumped behind a stack of hay bales before Jackson could swing his sights in his direction. The black farmer jacked a fresh cartridge into his repeater and slowly walked toward the wall of straw. Halfway there, he heard the crisp sound of a Winchester being primed. He fell to his belly a second before the nightrider rose above the topmost bale, blazing away with his .44-40. The bullets spun harmlessly over Jackson's head, kicking up earth a couple of feet behind him. In such a prone position, the farmer knew that it would be impossible to take aim with his rifle. Instead, he reached beneath his coat and withdrew an old Colt Army revolver. Elias's father, an escaped slave, had taken the gun off the body of a dead Union major shortly after the battle of Stones River. He now put the pistol to good use. He waited until the nightrider showed himself again, then aimed carefully. The revolver bucked with a belch of black-powder smoke, sending a round ball smashing into the bridge of the outlaw's nose and killing the man instantly.

A moment later Hinchburger and Jackson were busily cutting the farmers loose. The bewildered men took the flour sacks from off their heads and quickly armed themselves with guns they pried from the hands of the dead nightriders. As they all started toward the barn door, the creak of boards sounded over their heads. A rifle cracked from the hayloft above. Elias Jackson dropped to his knees, a slug ripping through his right side. "I've been shot!" he cried out.

Hinchburger and the others whirled, lifting their guns into line. A single nightrider who had been standing guard in the loft stood at the edge of the platform. He saw the arsenal directed at him and knew that he had made a grave mistake. He had no place to run as blued barrels belched flame and smoke. He was fairly ripped apart by the hail of bullets and buckshot that enveloped him.

As the farmers left the barn, carrying Jackson with them, Slocum and George Kelly left the farmhouse and joined them. Slocum's face creased with concern when he saw Jackson's bleeding form. "What happened?" he asked.

"We missed one in the loft and he got the drop on Elias here," said Will Sutherland. "The bullet went in one side and out the other, though. He'll be okay if we can stop the bleeding."

"If anyone can tend to him it would be his wife," said Hinchburger. "I say we take him back to the camp, then ride into town and finish this business once and for all."

Slocum agreed, as did the farmers. Sutherland and his fellow sodbusters climbed into the saddles of the nightriders' black horses, while Slocum and Hinchburger helped Elias Jackson onto his own horse. Then they, too, mounted up. Together, the posse of angry men headed south toward the banks of the Smoky Hill River.

21

The first light of dawn was breaking over the flat Kansas horizon when Slocum and the others approached the camp next to the river. But before they even reached their destination, they discovered that something was wrong. Elias Jackson's eldest boy darted from the shelter of a clump of high brush and waved them down, his face full of fear and worry.

"What's wrong, Thomas?" asked Hinchburger. He reined his horse to a halt and looked down at the ten-year-old boy.

"Two of them nightriders," said the youngster, breathing hard. "They came a couple hours after y'all left. Took Miss Prissy with 'em."

"Damn!" growled Slocum. He spurred his gelding and the others followed suit, riding on to the encampment on the northern bank of the Smoky Hill River.

When they reached the camp, they found the women and children standing around the fire. At the sight of their men, alive and uninjured, the families abandoned their night-long fears and rushed to embrace their husbands and fathers. Nettie Jackson cried out in alarm when she reached Elias's horse and found the black farmer incoherently clinging to his mount, his dark face ashen and gray.

She pulled the flap of his coat aside and was shocked at the amount of blood that stained his shirt underneath. "What happened to my Elias?" she demanded as Hinchburger and

Slocum helped the man down from the saddle.

"He caught a bullet from a nightrider we overlooked," said Hinchburger. "The bullet went clean through him, but he's lost a lot of blood."

The horror on Nettie's face suddenly turned into grim determination. "Take him over by the fire," she told the men. She turned to her son. "Thomas, run down to the riverside. Gather some cattail and moss, as well as berries from that gooseberry bush over yonder. Be quick about it. Your daddy's life depends on it."

The Negro boy nodded. "Yes'm," he said and went about the task of gathering the herbs necessary for his mother's healing potion.

When Elias had been laid out on a blanket next to the campfire, Nettie turned to Slocum. "Where's my husband's rifle?" she asked.

Slocum handed her the Spencer repeater. "What do you need it for?"

"Just need to heat up the barrel a mite," she told him. The woman worked the lever, jacking the unused cartridges from its tubular magazine, then stuck the barrel of the empty rifle deep down into the embers of the crackling fire.

Slocum turned to the wife of Will Sutherland. "What's this about Prissy being taken?"

"It's true," said Marjory Sutherland. "Luther Hicks and that man Guthrie rode up shortly after you'd left."

Slocum shook his head angrily. He had been afraid of something like this happening. Before leaving the abandoned farm, Slocum had checked beneath the masks of the nine nightriders they had left behind. Much to his disappointment, none of the bodies had belonged to Hicks or Guthrie. Obviously, they had split from the group and went out hunting for the families of the farmers after leaving the old Woodard place.

"Don't ask me how they came to find us," continued the woman. "All I know is they found out somehow. Anyway, Prissy held them at bay with that Colt pistol of her papa's. She was a hair away from shooting them clean out of their saddles when Hicks told her that she'd best not do it. They said that they had her father locked up somewhere and that he'd be killed for sure if she didn't come with them. She thought on the matter for a while, then decided that it was the best thing for her to do."

"They're taking her back to that ornery cuss of a judge," said Nettie as she placed the herbs and berries into a kettle of water and began to bring it to a boil over the campfire. "Everyone hereabouts knows Burke has had his eye on the poor girl, and he intends to have her, too, one way or another."

"Damn him for all the trouble he's caused us!" declared George Kelly. "I've turned the other cheek for way too long. I'm ready to ride into town and put an end to Burke's dishonesty!"

"We were hoping the U.S. marshal would take care of that problem for us," said Hinchburger. "But it doesn't look like he's going to show up. I reckon we'll end up doing it ourselves."

The gathering of farmers grew silent as Nettie Jackson went to work. She took the steaming kettle from off the fire and filled a tin cup with the brackish liquid. Her dark hands hesitated for a moment, then ripped her husband's shirt away, exposing the ugly bullet hole that traveled from his lower back to just right of his belly. "This is gonna hurt something awful," she warned her husband, then poured the hot liquid into the puncture in his back.

Elias bit back a scream of agony as the potion traveled through the wound and drained out the opposite side. Nettie looked up to see the same question in everyone's eyes. "It helps cleanse the wound," she told them.

Nettie then took the Spencer rifle from where it had lain partially in the fire. The tip of the barrel glowed red-hot. "This is gonna hurt even more," she told her husband softly. The black man nodded in understanding. Nettie laid the hot end of the gun barrel first against the hole in his back, then the one in his abdomen, cauterizing the nasty wounds and sealing them shut.

Elias let out a long, piercing scream, then passed out from the sheer pain of the burning. Nettie regretted having to resort to such extremes, but knew that it had to be done. She bent down and kissed her man gently on the forehead. "He'll live now," she said aloud.

The others nodded in silent respect. The woman's knowledge of folk medicine was surely a blessing, particularly for Elias Jackson. Nettie had taken a half dead man and given him another chance at life.

"I reckon we'd best be heading to town," Hinchburger suggested. "If Burke intends to force Prissy into marriage, he'll likely do it by twelve o'clock today. The Judge usually performs his ceremonies—trials, hangings, and such—at high noon."

"Then we'd best be riding," said George Kelly. "I swear, I'll see that bastard dead before I'd let him subject my daughter to such a sinful act!"

The women of the camp rustled up some cold biscuits and jerky for the men to eat during their brief journey to town, then Slocum and the others again swung atop their horses. Each man possessed the same expression of grim purpose as they started northward. It was clear to see that each one, farmer or otherwise, had had their fill of Burke and his bogus lawmen, and were more than ready to put an end to the humiliation and terror the Judge had subjected them to.

• • •

Prissy Kelly lay on a bunk of one of the courthouse's basement jail cells. She shivered against the chill that emanated from the dank stone walls and the heavy iron bars that confined her. The cell stank of mold, sweat, and old urine, and several times during the early morning she had seen bugs skitter across the ceiling over her head. The cellar was illuminated only by a single lamp hanging from a rafter in the corridor outside, and even then, the shadows of the adjoining cells seemed to soak up the light like a sponge in bathwater.

She was lying there, wondering where her father was being held and if he was even still alive, when the pale-eyed gunman named Guthrie made his way down the stone steps from the upper level of the courthouse. He grinned with crooked, tobacco-stained teeth as he took a ring of keys from his pocket and opened the door of her cell.

With a harsh chuckle, he tossed something at her. It was a lacy, white wedding dress. "The Judge said to put that on," he told her.

Prissy threw the garment to the floor, her eyes defiant. "Never!" she said. "Not for the likes of him!"

Guthrie took a threatening step into the cell, his eyes full of cruel amusement. "You put that dress on, or I'll strip you bare and put it on you myself. Of course, if I go that far, I'll likely help myself to you before I'm through. The Judge wouldn't be too happy about me defiling his new bride before the wedding, but then I really don't give a damn what that old cripple thinks."

Prissy glared at the man and knew that he was capable of carrying out his blatant threat of rape. Grudgingly she picked up the dress and laid it on the bunk.

"Yeah, I thought so," said Guthrie. He laughed coarsely as he slammed the door closed with a clang. "Oh, by the way, your nuptials will take place at noon. Nothing fancy. Just a simple ceremony in the Judge's chambers upstairs with a preacher and a few witnesses to make everything legal and binding."

"Get out of here!" yelled Prissy, her eyes brimming with tears at the thought of being sentenced to a life with a man like Hamilton Burke.

Guthrie laughed heartily and made his way back upstairs. Soon, she was alone again. Just her and the vermin and the clammy walls of stone and iron.

Prissy sat down on the bunk and wept. She wondered if she had made more of a mistake giving up her gun and coming here than if she had blasted both Hicks and Guthrie off their horses like she had originally intended. She had no way of knowing if she was saving her father's life by her forced agreement to wed the corrupt judge. For all she knew, her papa might have been tortured into signing over his deed, then killed immediately afterward.

The young woman's thoughts turned from her father to the only man who could have prevented such a fate at the hands of Burke's nightriders. She wondered where Slocum was at that moment and if he had survived the assault on the Woodard farm. Prissy closed her eyes, picturing the tall Southerner in her mind. She recalled the intimate times they had shared, both in the hayloft and the root cellar, the feel of his strong hands against her skin. She told herself that she was mistaken, but she knew that his constant place in her mind meant only one thing, and that was that she was falling in love with the man.

Prissy forced the idea from her thoughts, knowing that nothing would ever come of such a relationship. She was a farmer's daughter, accustomed to setting down roots in one place and hopeful of starting a household and bearing a brood of children. Slocum, on the other hand, was a drifter who had no anchor to domestic ways. She could not picture him giving up the freedom of the open trail for the responsibilities of a husband and father. He also had the air of someone who might be running from something. For all she knew, he could be a bank robber or a murderer dodging the law.

Faintly, beyond the walls of her cell, Prissy heard the courthouse clock chime the hour of ten. In two hours time she would be marched up the steps to the Judge's chamber and subjected to a union that, seemingly legal or not, could not be approved of in the eyes of God.

Resigned to her fate, Prissy wiped away her tears. Slowly she began to undress, feeling as if the lovely white dress she was about to wear was more like a burial shroud than a wedding gown.

22

A half hour before the strike of noon, Slocum and the others arrived in Tyler's Crossing.

They avoided the main street, approaching the livery stable from the south. Hinchburger opened the gate of the corral and the farmers led their coal-black horses through, then quickly dismounted and unsaddled the animals. As everyone assembled in the livery stable, Hinchburger checked the stalls. He was pleased to find Hicks's and Guthrie's horses in their customary spots. That meant that the two men were still in town.

"Is everyone ready?" Slocum asked.

The others nodded solemnly.

"Then let's go."

Hinchburger unbarred the front door of the livery, and together they left the stock barn. As one, they headed down the center of the main street, a weary but determined group of men who had suffered the injustice of a dictatorial judge one time too many. Slocum and Hinchburger led the way, but they were really only bystanders unwillingly caught up in the struggle that currently took place in Tyler's Crossing. The true players in the game were the dirt farmers—George Kelly, Will Sutherland, and the others. Their bruised and battered faces were set firmly in anger, their tolerance for Hamilton Burke's criminal actions having reached its breaking point. They were ready to put an end to his greedy ambitions, one way or another.

They passed the double rows of shops and businesses, until they approached the Plowman Saloon. When they reached the two-story establishment, Slocum noticed Charlene standing on the boarded sidewalk outside. When she spotted him among the group of men, she ran toward the tall Georgian, her eyes concerned. "Good Lord, John, where have you been? I was afraid you were dead!"

"I nearly was, thanks to Hicks and his men," he told her.

The blond saloon girl studied the ragtag group of farmers, some still dressed only in their nightshirts, but all carrying rifles, pistols, and shotguns. "I assume you're all here for one purpose," she said.

"That's right," Slocum told her. "We're going down to the courthouse to have it out with the Judge. Hicks and Guthrie, too."

"The Judge is planning to marry Prissy Kelly at noon," Charlene told them. "He wants me to be her maid of honor, can you believe that? I tried to refuse, but the Judge made it clear that he wanted me to attend. Guthrie is supposed to be here to escort me to the courthouse in a few minutes."

"We don't have time to wait around for him," said George Kelly. "We're going to settle this with the Judge right now, before he can lay a stinking hand on my daughter."

"Before you go down there, there's someone here in the saloon I think you should talk to," urged Charlene.

"We're done talking," said Will Sutherland. "Now we're ready to do something about the Judge and his crooked ways."

"Then this man can help you," said the saloon girl. "He just rode into town an hour ago."

The gathering of men looked at one another, puzzled but intrigued by Charlene's words. As they made their way across the sidewalk and toward the Plowman's swinging doors, Hinchburger broke away from the others. "I'll be back directly," he told them. Then, shotgun in hand, he disappeared down the alleyway next to the saloon.

Slocum and the others continued on their way into the drinking establishment. The place was empty of patrons, except for a tall, mustachioed man who stood at the bar, drinking coffee and eating his fill of biscuits and gravy. He was a rangy fellow, rawboned and leather-tough, who wore a high-peaked hat and gray suit that was covered with several days worth of trail dust. Slocum could tell that Henry, the bartender, stayed clear of the man. He stood at the far end of the bar, nervously polishing beer mugs with a filthy rag.

Slocum stepped away from the others and approached the lanky man with the long face and the handlebar mustache. "Pardon me, but this lady says I should talk to you," he said.

The man eyed Slocum with hard eyes. "Is your name John Smith?"

Slocum nodded, although it wasn't his true title.

"My name is Joe Austin," he said, extending a hand. As he performed the gesture, the man's coat lapel shifted enough to reveal a brass badge pinned to his vest. "I'm the U.S. marshal from Fort Atkinson. You sent me a telegram a few days back."

"Yes," agreed Slocum. "I did. We were wondering if you were going to come or not."

Marshal Austin eyed the gathering of men, taking in their battered faces and the guns they held purposefully in their fists. "Looks like it," he said. "Your wire said that the judge here in Tyler's Crossing has been up to no good. That he's been trying to extort money from the local farmers."

"That's right," said George Kelly, stepping forward. "And you can add a few more crimes to that list. Like kidnapping, arson, and attempted murder. The Judge has had his hand in them all."

"If what you say is true, I'll need to hear all the details," said the lawman. "Why don't you all sit down and tell me about it."

"We don't have the time," said Kelly. "Burke is about to marry my daughter against her will at noon. We've got to stop him before he gets the chance."

Abruptly everyone turned as the batwing doors opened with a clatter. In walked Hinchburger pushing Flanders the gambler ahead of him. He had the muzzles of his ten-gauge pressed against the back of the frightened man's neck.

"I figured someone might try to warn the Judge about us," said the liveryman. He shoved the gambler into one of the barroom chairs. "I found Flanders here sneaking out the back door, heading in the direction of the courthouse."

Joe Austin sipped his coffee and studied the faces of the men around him. He was a man who had a knack for telling truth from dishonesty, and he could tell by the mutual expression in their eyes they were not lying. Whatever Hamilton Burke had done to these men, it hadn't been behavior fitting of a legitimate judge. And if there was one thing the U.S. marshal couldn't tolerate, it was a man of law who abused his authority for power or greed.

"Is there any other sort of law in this town?" asked the marshal. "Maybe a sheriff who can be trusted?"

"That's a joke!" Hinchburger laughed. "Luther Hicks is the acting sheriff of Tyler's Crossing, but he's a disgrace to his office. He's the leader of Burke's nightriders. Him and his so-called deputies have been strong-arming everyone in town and using their badges to hide behind."

"I was afraid of that," said Austin with a grim frown. He was silent for a long moment, then he spoke. "All right," the marshal told them. "We'll all go down to the courthouse together . . . but not as a bloodthirsty mob. If this Judge Burke pays for his crimes, it's going to be by the law book and not by vengeful guns. From what I've heard, he'll likely hang for what he's done. If you go with me, you'll go as temporary deputies, legally sworn in. If not, I'll just have to go alone."

The gathering of farmers looked at one another, exchanging nods of acceptance. Then George Kelly spoke up. "We're prepared to do what it takes to put a stop to the Judge. Go on and swear us in."

Marshal Austin glanced at the clock at the head of the staircase. Its hands were inching toward the hour of twelve. "I'll make it brief," he said. "Raise your right hands." When the men had done so, he spoke out. "By the authority invested in me by the state of Kansas, I hearby deputize you."

"Is that it?" asked Will Sutherland.

"That's it," said Austin. "Now let's go down to the courthouse and place Hamilton Burke under arrest."

A moment later they left the Plowman Saloon. The main street was deserted as they made their way down the dusty thoroughfare to the big, red brick building at the far end of town. Joe Austin stared up at the second floor of the structure, where double doors and a whitewashed balcony overlooked the town square. The U.S. marshal could picture the Judge sitting up there, keeping a watchful eye over Tyler's Crossing like some medieval squire appraising his kingdom. Austin had encountered power-hungry men like Burke in the past and hated them for the way they took the law and twisted it in order to acquire political power or financial gain.

The Kansas marshal and his band of deputies were just approaching the courthouse steps when the door opened and Guthrie stepped out. Apparently, he was on his way to get Charlene for the wedding. By the look of shock in his pale blue eyes, it appeared that Guthrie was totally unprepared for the crowd of men that blocked his way.

Before Austin could say a word, Guthrie panicked. He drew a hogleg Colt from a crossdraw holster and began to blaze away. The first slug nailed the marshal in the right arm, spinning him on his heels. The other shots went into the crowd, killing one farmer instantly and injuring a couple more.

He didn't get a chance to fire a fourth time, however. Hinchburger lifted his ten-gauge and emptied both barrels. The double blasts nearly ripped Guthrie in half at the belly. His revolver spun from his hand, the force of the buckshot slamming him backward through the wooden panels of the sturdy oak door.

Slocum crouched next to the U.S. marshal. Austin was lying on his back, his face pale. "How bad is it?" he asked.

"Went in my arm," muttered the injured lawman. He clutched the bullet wound in his upper bicep tightly, stemming the flow of blood. "It's up to you now. Try to arrest Burke and his sheriff, but if they resist, do whatever you have to."

"We'll see that justice is done," Slocum assured him. Then, gathering the others, they walked through the shattered doorway of the courthouse, stepping over Guthrie's shot-riddled body as they went.

Like a stampede, they stormed across the lobby and up the stairway to the second story. When they reached the top of the stairs, they spotted Luther Hicks standing at the far end of the hallway. He stood with his back to the door of the Judge's chambers. Slocum motioned for the others to stop. "Let me handle him," he said.

Slocum slipped the thong off the hammer of his Colt Navy and began to walk toward the burly man. He noticed that Hicks was wearing a low-slung gunbelt, each holster on his hip cradling a big .44 Dragoon. Hicks's arms were crossed, but it would only take a quick movement on his part to let his hands dip down and snatch the revolvers from their sleeves. Slocum recalled the fast draw Hicks had displayed during their daylight trip to the Woodard place and knew that the man was twice as deadly with two guns as one.

But he couldn't bring himself to back down. No matter how badly the odds stacked up, he had to face Luther Hicks. The anger that had kept him alive during those difficult days when he was stranded at the abandoned farm began to return. And he knew in his heart that only one of them would be leaving the upstairs corridor alive. He just hoped to God that it was he who remained standing.

"So you are alive!" said Hicks with a coarse laugh. "Leave it to you to weasel your way out of Death's grip more than once in a lifetime. I should've put a bullet in your brain pan when I had the chance."

"Yes," Slocum told him coldly. "You should have."

"You might as well turn around and leave, Slocum," warned the bogus sheriff. "When the Judge heard that gunfire downstairs, he decided to start the wedding earlier than planned. He's gonna marry Prissy Kelly and that's all there is to it."

Slocum stopped halfway down the hallway, the heat of rage flaming in his eyes. "Step away from that door, Hicks."

Hicks grinned broadly. "What's the matter, Slocum? Did that pistol-whipping I gave your head do something to your hearing? I said they're not to be disturbed."

Slocum smiled, too, but it was a smile as humorless as that of a sun-bleached skull. "You'd best not tempt fate like your men have. Guthrie's dead and so are your damned nightriders. You've had a hand in trying to kill me twice in the past. I sure won't give you a third chance."

Hicks took a menacing step away from the doorway, his arms still folded across his broad chest. "I think you've forgotten who you're dealing with."

"I know," said Slocum. "I just don't care."

"Then so be it," said Hicks. Then, like the strike of a rattler, his arms were dropping downward, his open hands fisting around the curved butts of the twin Dragoons.

Slocum prayed that he would be faster and he was, if only by a hairbreadth. He shucked his Navy pistol from its holster and extended it at arm's length just as Hicks's guns cleared leather. He fired a single shot, punching a neat, round hole into the left pocket of the man's chambray shirt.

Hicks staggered back a couple of steps and looked down dumbly at the bullet wound directly over his heart. "Damn you, Slocum!" he growled and began to lift his own revolvers.

Slocum did not hesitate. He fired again, this time choosing his aim more carefully. The .36-caliber pistol bucked in his hand, belching smoke and fire and fast lead. Hicks's head rocked back on his shoulders with the impact of the bullet. The slug entered the man's forehead squarely between his eyes, then exited in an ugly spray of bone splinters and brain matter from the back of his skull.

Already dead, Luther Hicks fell backward. The weight of his body knocked the door open and he fell inside, drawing a scream of alarm from Prissy. Through the doorway, Slocum could see Prissy standing there, dressed in a lacy white dress, her face as drawn and pale as the material of her wedding gown. Next to her sat Hamilton Burke in his wheelchair. He was decked out in a black frock coat and bow tie, but still wore the vest with the two pepperbox pistols protruding from the pockets. Standing before them was a chubby, perspiring minister who looked, at that moment, to possess more fear of the Judge than he did for his heavenly master.

"Come on!" yelled Slocum. He ran down the hallway toward the Judge's chambers, Hinchburger and the farmers following close behind.

• • •

The wedding ceremony was halfway finished when the door of the office burst inward, spilling Hicks's dead body across the threshold. The Judge's stony eyes shot toward the hallway beyond. He could see the man he knew to be John Slocum start toward them, a Colt Navy fisted in his hand. Behind him was a mob made up of those he had victimized over the past few months.

For the first time in years, Hamilton Burke felt the thrill of pure fear course through him. Since arriving in Kansas and acquiring the judicial seat in Tyler's Crossing, he had always been protected by his hired guns. But, now, no such protection stood between him and those who wanted him dead. It was just he and them, face-to-face.

He drew his nickel-plated pepperboxes from their pockets and began to fire toward the open doorway. The first two shots caught the preacher, who had nervously wandered into his line of fire. The man of God fell to his knees with a moan, his belly punctured by the small-caliber bullets. Burke fired again, but Slocum and the others had reached the cover of the hallway's adjoining offices.

"Damn it to hell!" growled the Judge. All that he had worked toward since leaving the squalor of the South and setting up shop in Kansas was quickly slipping through his fingers. Those he had terrorized and attempted to extort money and land from were out for his blood. The only option he had left was escape. He spun his wheelchair around and headed for the double doors behind his desk and the balcony beyond.

Hamilton Burke threw open the doors and rolled out into the hot sunlight of high noon just as Slocum and the others entered his office. He reached the railing of the balcony and stared down at the street below. For some reason the porch seemed much higher than it ever had before. But he had no choice. He had to attempt it.

Ignoring the angry voices and the pounding footsteps of the mob behind him, the Judge stuck his pistols back into his vest pockets and grabbed hold of the edge of the decorative banister. Using all his strength, he lifted himself out of his chair and began to heave himself over the top. He had some difficulty pulling his dead legs up over the edge of the railing, but he finally managed to, the adrenaline of pure panic and fear giving him the strength to do so.

"Burke!" called a familiar voice behind him.

He turned his head and saw George Kelly standing in the doorway, his battered face full of hatred. He could see the blood lust in the elderly farmer's eyes; the need to put an end to the man who had harassed him, burned his farm, and abducted his daughter. Burke reached for the pearl handle of one of his pepperboxes, but Kelly had already lifted his Henry into line. The muzzle of the repeater barked only once. The rifle slug hit Burke in the rib cage, slicing completely through his abdomen and exiting through the opposite side. The force of the gunshot drove the Judge over the railing. With a shrill screech, he dropped fifteen feet to the hard-packed earth of the street below.

He hit the ground on his back, the impact snapping one of his shoulder blades in half and driving the wind from his lungs. He struggled for breath, trying to ignore the sharp pain in his back as he rolled over. He looked toward the livery stable at the far end of town, but it seemed to be a million miles away.

The Judge was attempting to lift himself up with one arm when he heard a voice from only a few yards away. "Hamilton Burke, you're under arrest!"

He twisted his head to see a tall, lanky man sitting on the courthouse steps. The fellow was wounded in one arm, but the other worked well enough, and in that hand he held a long-barreled Colt Peacemaker. Burke also caught the flash of metal on the man's vest. He knew the badge of a federal marshal when he saw one. Burke suddenly knew why the man was there and knew that he had absolutely nothing to lose.

The Judge dropped to his side and drew one of his pistols. He extended the fancy pepperbox at arm's length, ready to fire at the lawman. But he never received the chance. The marshal's .44 roared first. The bullet struck Burke in the center of the chest, knocking him flat on his back. Instantly he knew that it was over for him. He fought to breathe or move, but could not.

As his torn heart beat its last, Hamilton Burke stared upward at the balcony overhead. Gathered on the platform above him was Slocum, George Kelly, and the others. He expected them to laugh and cheer as his life ebbed away. But they didn't. They simply stared down at him, their faces grim.

Then, with a violent shudder, the Judge felt himself slip away. A pall of darkness swept over him, and for the citizens of Tyler's Crossing, the threat of Hamilton Burke was no more.

23

As Marshal Joe Austin left his place on the courthouse steps and walked toward the still body of Hamilton Burke, Slocum broke away from the others and stepped back into the Judge's chambers.

He was searching through the drawers of Burke's big curly maple desk when Hinchburger noticed his urgency. He stepped back into the room, eyeing Slocum curiously. "What are you doing?"

Slocum turned toward the man. He debated on whether or not he should tell Hinchburger of his past. But he knew he could trust the liveryman. Hinchburger had put his neck on the line in helping the farmers fight Judge Burke, as well as concealing Slocum's true purpose for joining Hicks's nightriders. He couldn't believe that the man would turn on him now, especially since their war against Burke had been won.

"I'm looking for a wanted poster," said Slocum. "One with my name and description on it."

"So I figured right," said Hinchburger. "You are a fugitive."

"Wrongfully accused," Slocum assured him. "A judge much like Burke tried to cheat my land away from me back in Georgia. I warned him to leave my property, but he refused. He paid for his trespassing with his life."

Hinchburger nodded. He understood the lengths a man would go to in order to preserve what was rightfully his.

"When Luther Hicks tied me to that windmill out on the Woodard place, he told me that the Judge had dug up a poster on me," said Slocum. "I've come across men like that marshal out there. Austin is a sharp man. Once he gets that arm fixed up, he'll go through the Judge's private papers, just to make sure that the man was as crooked as everyone claimed him to be. And if there is a wanted poster with my name on it around here, he'll be sure to find it. Then he won't have any other choice than to arrest me."

Hinchburger helped Slocum search the desk, but they found nothing. There were a couple of bottom drawers that were locked, and more than likely, Burke had the keys to both in his vest pocket. They considered forcing the drawers open, but knew that such an action would only rouse the suspicion of the farmers who congregated on the balcony outside. And Slocum didn't want them to know that he was a man wanted by the law if he could possibly help it.

"I reckon there's only one thing left to do," said Slocum after their quick search of Burke's desk had proven futile.

"I'm afraid so," said Hinchburger. "Your horse is still saddled and ready to go." The liveryman extended a burly band. "Don't worry about Austin. I'll do what I can to cover your tracks."

Slocum shook the man's hand. "I'm obliged to you," he said. Then, before the others could notice, he ducked out of the office and made his way downstairs.

He was in the corral at the rear of the livery stable, tightening the belly strap of his gelding's saddle, when he sensed someone at the gate behind him. Slocum laid his hand on the butt of his Navy Colt, but knew whoever was there would cause him no trouble. From his days of recovering in the root cellar under the Kelly house, Slocum had come to learn the soft fall of her footsteps, as well as the swish of her shirt as she walked.

"John," called Prissy softly.

Slocum turned to find the farm girl closing the gate behind her. Prissy stood there for a moment, looking like an earthbound angel in the frilly wedding gown that Judge Burke had forced her to wear. She was lovely, despite what she had been put through that day. Slocum felt his heart ache at the very sight of her. He fought with the feeling, wrestling the emotion until it was locked away deep down inside him. He had to leave Tyler's Crossing and that was all there was to it.

Prissy ran across the manure-strewn corral until she fell into Slocum's arms. The tall Georgian held her reluctantly, closing his eyes so he would not see the delicate beauty of her face.

"Hinchburger told me you were leaving," said Prissy. "Why?"

"Because I don't belong here, Prissy," he told her gently. "I'm afraid you only know one side of me. There are things you don't know."

"I don't care," assured Prissy.

"Maybe not," said Slocum. "But I do. I couldn't burden you with the truth of what I've done in the past."

Tears streamed down Prissy's face. "But I care deeply for you, John. And I think you feel the same for me, don't you?"

Slocum said nothing. The pain in his strong face answered her question. "I'm sorry, Prissy, but I have to go. Right now."

Prissy hung her head in sad resignation. "I know. I reckon I've known all along." She looked up at him, angry frustration blazing in her wet eyes. "But it isn't fair."

"No," agreed Slocum. "It's not. That's for damn sure."

He leaned down and gave Prissy a parting kiss. It was a slow, lingering kiss, one filled with much pain, but no regret. Slocum pulled away from the young woman before their embrace could grow more passionate. Quickly he turned and mounted his horse.

"Take care, John," said Prissy. The brunette choked back her tears and stood tall. "I'll keep you in my prayers."

Slocum admired the woman's courage. "Good-bye, Prissy," was all he could bring himself to say. Then he reined his spotted gelding around and headed across the corral.

After exiting the gate, he headed south toward the Smoky Hill River. Slocum didn't look back. He wanted to put as much distance as possible between himself and Tyler's Crossing. He wanted nothing more than to forget about Judge Hamilton Burke and Luther Hicks, as well as all the trouble their marauding nightriders had caused him.

And, more than anything else, Slocum wanted to put the memory of Prissy behind him. He wanted to erase the beauty of her eyes, the satiny softness of her skin, and the music of her voice.

But he knew that would be the hardest task of all.

A special offer for people who enjoy reading the best Westerns published today.

WESTERNS!

NO OBLIGATION

Mail the coupon below

To start your subscription and receive 2 FREE WESTERNS, fill out the coupon below and mail it today. We'll send your first shipment which includes 2 FREE BOOKS as soon as we receive it.